Tails of the Singers

By Alice E. Wright

Published By Picky Press

Cover pencil art by Virginia Cleary used with paid permission.

Cover design by Sue Case.

Our books may be purchased in bulk for promotional, educational, or business use. Contact your local retailer, or contact the author directly at thesiberiancat@yahoo.com.

Print ISBN: 9781643949932

EBook ISBN: 9781643949925

Library of Congress Control Number: 2022922738

www.kendersiberiancats.com

Published by Picky Press, an imprint of Tovim Press, LLC. Phoenix, Arizona, USA.

PickyPress.com

There are certain scenes in this fictional series of
tales that some readers may find upsetting,
including death and pain.

"I believe cats to be spirits come to Earth. A cat, I am sure, could walk on a cloud without coming through."

– Jules Verne

Story Selections

Story 1

And So It Began

The temple's stone steps were kept clean and clear. Every day the appointed acolyte would use a rush broom to make sure the steps into the temple were free of debris in the morning. However, cats came and went at all times. They had no set schedule. The Goddess demanded that they be permitted free reign as her incarnations of form. To harm one of her cats is to betray her, and a crime. The perpetrator, depending on the severity of offense, would even be killed by palace guards covered in cat skins while using spears. The priests would pray to her day and night for her many beneficial gifts, on behalf of the multitude of people from the great metropolis. They would pray for fertility in all things, their families, their cattle and even their crops. They would pray to win a legal battle against their neighbor; to win at games. And they would pray for guidance, for mercy, for the safe passage to the underworld for themselves and their beloved pet cats.

The temple rests on a large piece of land surrounded on three sides by a smooth large lake. It is believed that the Goddess' rage and anger was cooled down by the waters in the lake over the eons, and this turned her from the ferocious lioness into the gentle domesticated cat. Around the temple in Bubastis, Egyptians even took to mummifying their dead cats in honor of Bast. Such was the importance and reverence of cats–that mummified cats were buried close to their human caretakers. Only when properly mummified, could the souls of all travel on to be with their goddess.

In her early days as the daughter of Ra, Bast was a fierce warrior. She had the power to vanquish all threats from evil spirits. But most importantly, she became the protector of the dead. Bast would travel with the souls of the dead to the underworld, on her father Ra's great barge named the Boat of a Million Years. Here, she would protect all onboard from the many threats of the lost and vile souls before permitting her safely-guarded ones the reward of entering the underworld. Once in the underworld, those souls would then be judged by the jackal god Anubis. But time marches on, civilizations change, and eventually she was civilized down to be a beloved deity with the power to protect against diseases–particularly those in women and children. In time, worshipers were fewer, and the temple held less sway over the people.

Our Mistress' final defeat came when Cambyses II of Persia came into the Egyptian's lands and readily conquered. Not by might, not by strength, and not by superior force. Rather, he painted cats on all of his army's shields, believing the worshipers of Bast would find it difficult to attack his army. In addition to this, he set loose hundreds of cats he had collected from his lands, onto the battlefield in a gambit that the Egyptians would be so terrified of hitting one of the cats or even striking an image of one, that they either surrendered on the spot or were cut down. This proved to be true. Bast's worshipers were true to their goddess and would not permit the cats to be harmed, thereby giving leave for this invading army to conquer them.

Bast had seen all of this and she had wept. Once a fierce, battle-ready goddess, she had grown to be peace loving and caring over millennia. But never again she swore. She would remain the protector of the dead, as her father had tasked her to be. Bringing her devoted warriors, and those seeking the underworld to her and into her loving care. But she was done with this world of man. And so, she called and sang to all of her children and they responded by gathering to her temple. And here, before the monster who was Cambyses II could spread his troops further and desecrate her temple as he had desecrated the temple of Apis the sacred bull, did Bast gather all of her children.

The cats came from far and wide at hearing her song. The temples steps were thick with the felines from all the surrounding lands in all sizes, colors and patterns. Before them Bast stood, on two human legs with her two human hands and her full black coated shoulders and head. She speaks to her feline children, for they are all her children in form and in heart. She tells them to run from this place, that it is no longer safe. But all is not lost. She is gifting her children, so none can debate her greatness, generosity and devotion. So long as one of her children, children's children or further children live, then so too she shall not despair.

They now must carry forth her work on this plane. To be Singers for all the souls who cross over. To aid every soul who wishes to come to her on Ra's great barge so she may guide them over. It is now their job to know those souls as death approaches, to feel it, to see it, and to sense it. Every soul is precious and must go on. To remain is a wicked and evil thing, and twists the soul into a blackness that can't be saved.

It is now your turn to travel the world, to stay near man, but apart. Never to be a sycophant as Anubis' children have become. To keep man and the world safe through your hunting and killing of vermin, but to never let them rule you. For only she, the Goddess, was their true leader. Your wings will give you power and mark you as true descendants of Bast. Your Song will call to me from the underworld to open a portal. And so it shall be, our Goddess said. And so it has been always.

When Egypt fell, we were there to Sing. When Rome fell, we were there to Sing. When the world was covered in water, we were there to Sing. When the men went to war for their gods time and time again, we were there to Sing.

When new lands were discovered and conquered, we were there to Sing. Even through the blackest of nights when man would kill us on sight, we were there to Sing. We are time immeasurable. We are the Singers.

Rayla looks at her special baby. A gift, she knows from the Goddess. She knows she is heard both by her baby and her ruler. Mother and child can already speak to one another, while the other kittens in her litter do not, nor do they have the nubs growing at the shoulder that belay the oncoming of the gift that are wings. The Singer baby hears the Song over and over, learning its magic and heritage, while the other babies just hear the purr of their mother and snuggle closely knowing they are safe and loved. Rayla stretches her wings one at a time, in the small bunny hole she has procured for herself and her babies. The Goddess smiles up at them showering them with warmth and safety. And another generation is brought forth.

Story 2

A Baby Born

The wee baby had been born earlier today but was too small to fuss and too sickly to complain. He hadn't even cried to announce his own entry into the world. The small home, more a hut, showed how poor the family within was. Its dirt floors and roughly-hewn flax cloth door and window coverings, all to guard them from the outside elements. It was cold and damp and miserable. And all inside knew the baby wouldn't make it. The black miasma that heralded death had been hanging over this tiny abode for a few days now.

The feline gently slipped inside not even disturbing the rough cloth window covering or the small family within. The man and older child slept together for warmth on a dirty pallet on the floor, next to the low peat fire. The woman, although cold, had fallen asleep mostly curled around a loosely woven basket holding the sickly infant. The feline pads softly to the edge of the basket and sits so as not to disturb the woman or her family until the time is right.

The baby is tiny. His skin is translucent and purple veins pulse unevenly. Each breath is labored and gurgling in his chest.

"It is always a great sadness to be set to oversee this task," the Singer thinks. But a wandering soul can't find its peace, and over time turns into something bitter, angry and even dangerous. She knows her task is one of peace and mercy. Sadly, most of these uneducated folks know when they hear her Song, that a death is coming.

Most think it is the banshee who brings the death with it, and few if any, make the connection between the gentle soft cat and an other-worldly spirit. In reality it is she, one of the Singers who heralds the souls onto the next world, once they have been released from their no longer breathing bodies. Without her, those souls would be trapped here forever.

The Song as always, begins softly. Any of nature's creatures hearing it, know its purpose and temporarily settle themselves to permit the Song to guide the young soul over to peace. It is always a somber thing to help such a fragile and young soul to cross over. The infant takes its last pained breath and releases his soul into the night. Momentarily confused and lost, it hangs in the air as if unsure what to do now. The Singer's quiet Song gains strength and guides the little light to the slight ripple in the space between them that shimmers otherwise unseen. Eagerly, gratefully the soul passes through and the Song comes to its natural conclusion. The other creatures begin to stir once again knowing the task has been successfully completed. By now, the hovels occupants have heard and been awakened by the last remnants of the Song.

A sharp wail pierces the night as the young mother has awakened just in time to watch the last breath and soul leave her precious newborn. Quickly hiding her wings back along her sides, the small feline steps up to rub against the distraught mother in sympathy and comfort. Thinking to herself, maybe she will stay a while longer and watch over this poor family. The tired grief-stricken mother begins her keening as her small family gathers around her.

Story 3

Peace

The little black cat was tired. So very tired. She just had a litter of babies and they were early. She herself was malnourished to begin with, but the drain of having babies made it worse. One of her babies she knows, is special. More so than any ordinary cat. She would be a Singer if she could manage to grow up. The young mother knows she has to find food and quickly, but leaving her kits alone is risky. The rat population was out of control and getting worse every day. Those wretched beasts were everywhere these days, and certainly not beyond stealing her precious little newborns. The human population didn't seem to understand the situation they had created by declaring cats and dogs "illegal". The rats had rejoiced by becoming so populous that there was simply no way to control them. And with the rats came death. Evil, insidious, painful death in the form of the vermin they bring with them. Once the Pope declared cats to be evil and the population fell in line, it was only a matter of time before that same population suffered the results of their foolishness as well. And those results were grisly.

Great tumors grew rapidly impeding movement, giving pain and vomiting, then even the limbs would turn black and die before the rest of the body realized it too was soon dead. Once contracted, the humans were abandoned to die in their own filth and misery. They called it the black death but what it really was, was plague.

The little black cat had a tougher time than most. For a while, cats that were white or red or even striped were still beloved pets and kept in households. She wasn't so lucky. She had no home and no human protector, for she was born solid black as the starless night. And all who saw her knew she was bad luck or worse, in league with a witch somewhere. She had never known a kind word or soft hand. She had traveled the streets keeping to the shadows and had seen the other kitties in window boxes and doorways who were safe, fat, warm and dry. She wondered how that would feel, but never wondered for too long for fear of being seen and hurt.

Now, here she was all alone, but still responsible for four additional little lives. More than half-starved herself with more mouths to feed. After giving birth, she had stayed and fed her babies for a short while, keeping them warm and dry in the underside of an abandoned hovel where the remains of its poor owners still sat and rotted away. Even the rats didn't come in here any longer except to cross on the top rafters to the other buildings above.

When she had first stumbled upon this small room, she had been afraid. But the occupants had died long ago, and the rats had long since fed and left. All that remained now was an upturned chair, a tipped coal bucket, and the narrow cot with the rapidly mummifying remnants of remains. But it was dry from the almost daily rains that came to this part of the country and blocked the wind. It was more than she could have hoped for. Creeping out to the dangerous city streets, she pads down to the docks, hoping for a bit of fish or squid. She can usually find something even if it has to be hard won, chewed from an old cage or rope; it's something in her stomach.

Heading to the closest tethered boat, she sticks close to the shadows until something catches her eye. There on the railing of the boat are three cats. A bit narrow of body but not thin. Cream in color with darker tipping on their feet and ears are all three, sitting there watching the loading of the vessel. Slinking closer, she can smell at least one of them is a Singer. What a miracle this could be! Her breathing comes faster as she makes up her mind to take the risk. The boat is being hurriedly resupplied so as not to stay here in this affected port city any longer than absolutely necessary before making their way back up the English coast and to safer waters.

The little black cat manages to get close without being seen or at least no one seems to care if they did see her. "Excuse me," she calls to the trio on the rail. "Please, please, I beg of you. Will you help me?" The taller of the three peers down at her. Her jewel-blue eyes intimidating in their intensity. Before the Singer can respond, little Ava continues on, knowing that her time is very limited, both to plead her case and to be out in the open like this. "Please Miss, I just gave birth and one of my children is of special type, like you. She just can't be raised here and I can't teach her. Please will you take her?" The larger adult female peers around, making sure no human is paying attention to their conversation; her tail flicking in agitation.

"It would be unlikely any kit of yours would be a Singer," she responds. Her two daughters, looking so much like her as to be molded from the same painter's canvas, look nervously around them as well.

"Oh, but she is Singer, I promise! I am young and simple, but not unknowing. Please take her with you and save her!" Ava is panting with nervous fear–not only from being found out, but of losing this opportunity to save at least one of her children.

The trio above her are silent, for so long Ava is sure that she has wasted her precious time. She must find fresh water soon; she is very thirsty. And she hasn't yet eaten either. The birthing and first nursing took a lot out of her precious few resources.

"Fine, bring the kit here and if she is Singer, I will adopt her," the mature Singer says. Her two daughters seem to practically gasp in shock, having never heard of such a thing. But being too well brought up, they simply look from one another back to their mother. Little Ava can hardly believe her ears, and without even an acknowledgment, she races off into the streets, uncaring who might see her now.

Her mad dash changes to caution as she nears the entry of the tiny hovel. She can smell a fresh rat and the hair on her neck and shoulders instinctively rises. Her tail goes straight up and her approach becomes stiff and wary. There is indeed a rat roaming around the room, sticking its little whiskered nose into the various holes and dark places. A growl low in her throat brings the rodent's attention firmly onto her. It is only slightly smaller than she is, and definitely more well-fed.

Raising up on his rear feet, the rat is nearly as tall as Ava, and begins hissing at her. Ava does her best to slash and grab at the agitated rodent while trying to back out of the room drawing him away. Her kittens are starting to move about and she can hear them making tiny soft squeaking noises. Trying to not let it distract her, she smacks the rat again and again while avoiding gnashing teeth, drawing it away from the room and out into the road.

Finally managing to draw him off, she turns and runs a short distance down the alleyway. The rat grows distracted when she gets too great a distance, and goes over to a broken pot to nose around there.

Feeling she's succeeded in safeguarding her little brood for a short while, Ava returns quickly to her hidden corner. Sniffing the small bodies, she finds she has one less to worry about. Birth and fate have determined this little one's time was short. Ava grabs up her Singer baby, who even so young has snuggled up to the poor lifeless remains as if to offer comfort. Startled, the baby Singer cries out, but Ava has to hurry if she is going to make the ship before it casts off and she loses her one opportunity.

Carrying a baby is hard work for such a small and tired kitty but she manages to make the trip nonetheless. Her one driving need is to see her special baby have a chance at a better life.

Arriving back on the dock, her heart sinks. The mooring lines have been brought in and the gangway has been pulled in. The three Singers are no longer on the railing. Ava stops dead in her tracks in the middle of the road. Even on her best day she couldn't make such a tall jump, and certainly not with a baby in her mouth to weigh her down. Shock takes hold. She is frozen in place.

From behind a stack of barrels, one of the daughters steps out and motions to Ava. Ava looks at the daughter then back to the ship. She has no idea what this young Singer has in mind, but clearly, she has a plan. Stepping up to the beautiful sleek cat, Ava places her precious bundle on the ground. Reenya sniffs her over once, then nods her head at Ava.

There are men calling back and forth, the ship is getting ready to depart. Reenya looks Ava directly in the eyes, holding her in place for what seems like an eternity. Neither blinking nor moving, not even a tail twitching between them.

At some unheard cue, Reenya breaks eye contact, grabs the tiny baby who is much smaller in her mouth and unfurls her full iridescent wings. Running into the road, she turns and runs straight for the stack of barrels. Leaping with breathtaking agility, first to one then another and at the third one, her wings give her lift and she is able to propel herself the remaining distance, using her wings to lighten her weight and give her buoyancy onto the sailing vessel as it slowly begins to leave the dock and the city.

Ava is awestruck by what she just saw. But reality soon crashes down around her as a dock hand makes an attempt to kick her. Now that the stress and shock is over and her baby is safely away, she attempts to dodge the crude kick but it just barely catches her hips sending her sailing across the cobblestones to land harshly. Finally noticing that she is bleeding from a couple of bite wounds on her front legs, she makes her slow, painful way back to her place of safety, forgetting to either eat or drink.

Once there, not bothering to clean or tend her wounds, she curls up with her solitary remaining breathing kitten who no longer makes any squeaks or movement. The other two little lifeless lumps are now cold. She drifts into sleep dreaming of having a warm and safe place to lay, maybe curled up by a hearth with a warm fire. Dry and safe and loved.

The wind picks up outside along with a driving rain, dropping the temperatures. But Ava no longer worries about such things.

Reenya makes it back onto the deck of the ship where her sister and mother await her. The poor little orphan she brought with her is cold and hungry and in need of care. "What did you tell that poor wretched soul when you caught her in your gaze?" her sister asks. Their mother, Stardust, takes the baby from her to go below deck to begin trying to save it.

Reenya replies to Seela's question. "I knew she was dying. I gave her peace. Don't we all deserve some peace?"

Story 4

Salem's Tale

The poor family begged in the dirt streets. The father took what odd work came his way. The mother was of a disagreeable sort that most disliked, so what work there might have been, if any, was often saved for the other unfortunate souls in the town.

She had become bitter through life's trials. She had been born into a measure of wealth, but upon her father's death, that safety had been whisked away from her. With no will, a surviving wife, two sons and six additional daughters, there was little enough to go around, but her mother's new husband didn't find it within his generosity to give any of the daughters a dowry. Being 16, she was quietly married off to an indentured servant. The small spit of land given to her by her father's estate was even then taken from her upon her husband's death the next year by creditors, to whom her now deceased husband had owed. In this Puritan society, she was the lowest of the low.

Amazingly, she had managed to find a second suitable husband, and soon after gave birth to a lovely little girl. They called the child "Dorothy". She was a sweet thing, bright eyed and blond.

This is where I come into the story. I am a Singer; a special creature; some would say magical, others evil. I help souls from the recently or soon-to-be-deceased to cross over into the next realm. I can feel it as far as a few days ahead of time, and so thereby know where to go and whom to watch. From the day she was born, this poor little child carried the feel and discomfiture of death with her. I stayed near the family for weeks following them through the town, from home to home, waiting for the sad moment a mother first realizes her child has stopped suckling. But the weeks soon turned into months and the little child grew. I think the fact of the mother having such a young infant was a boon to this small family for the giving of mercy and charity.

It was a strikingly cold winter and many families felt pity for the infant, if not for the mother. The father helped with work as he could find it, but truly he is not germane to this story, except in a short while.

Days turned into months, then years. The child grew in poverty but was happy enough. I saw to it that the family had upon occasion, a small rabbit to fill their bellies with, or a partridge or two.

The mother also grew during this time, but what grew and festered in her was bitterness at her turn of station, and what she believed to be her husband's lack of ability to provide in a more suitable manner.

During times where the little Dorothy is left to her own devices, I sneak myself in and strop my feline body on her, purr in her ear and be a playful companion. Cats be not pets here, but we are neither killed nor abused. As long as we kill a few rodents, the town's population seems to feel a general apathy towards us, and we in them for the most part. Unless of course it is snowing, then we all find ways to sneak in to warm fires along roof beams.

Today I can't find the child or her family. I wander throughout the town, checking the usual tavern barn they often take refuge in, and the stalls of the market that often show them compassion and charity. I have no luck. It is very concerning to me, for little Dorothy often looks to me for warmth and comfort when her parents are less than mindful.

Finally, as I get a bit more frantic, the local tom cat approaches me. He is big for a cat. His brown coat has a burnished hue to it with a white tip on each massive foot. I know this male as Jedidiah. Not a Singer, but instead the dominant tom around town generally in the care and favor of the wealthy Parrish family. He is a strong and confident mouser, which gives him a special place at their hearth during the worst of the winter's storms.

"She is not here Singer. They took the mother this morning, accused of witchcraft. The father and child trailed behind," he informs me. Looking at me, I can read his sadness and pity and something else, though I'm not entirely sure what.

"Thank you," I replied, turning my tail towards the jail that Salem Village has devised recently in the spate of fear being perpetrated upon it.

"Sister Singer, do not go! It is too dangerous now, even for me. Keep your distance from that family. Had you done your job and taken that child when you were called, we may not be in this situation." A deep growl starts in the back of my throat and I spread my wings, arcing them forward in a threatening manner.

"Quiet your tone with me! All of us know when you took pity on that child and refused to release her soul when you were called, you profaned Her work."

I cease my indignation and become quiet. How could he know that since that time, my refusal to take this single child's soul, Bast had stopped talking to me? I have had no further forewarnings, and was left to run around after the villagers' deaths to collect and Sing on their souls. Salem Village is only a poor farming community, they say ten miles from the more prosperous and heavily-populated Salem Town, and I the only Singer in it. I had been born a ship's cat and traveled as a kitten, but was soon traded off to this life with another small child who had also grown and then forgotten about me. I stayed here, because there were no others and it seemed I could be of the most good. But I had betrayed my calling with this child. The child's mother at first had been happy to have the Singer stay near them, as if she herself were a good omen. No vermin were permitted to bother them at night, although they often stayed in local barns and sheds. I had kept the child warm on the coldest of nights and Sarah had even smiled at me a time or two when my gifts of rabbit or ptarmigan were desperately needed.

She wasn't a bad woman. But she was a bitter and morose woman. The village folk went from looking at her with pity and care to loathing and eventual fear. The accusation of being a witch was thrown around because of her short temper and more vile nature. And as her reputation suffered, so too did her small family. And this morning, in early March 1692, they took the mother Sarah Goode into custody on the charge of witchcraft. Now, mere weeks later they have taken the child as well. She is a tiny thing at four years of age.

How can I have let this happen? What can I do? They interrogate her for two weeks and I can't gain access to their prison. It is too dangerous for me. For now, the people believe a witch can turn into a cat. Such nonsense, but to be seen with one would certainly mean the death of them all.

The summer comes and I cautiously make my way into the new underground jail that they have sent several of their prisoners to, many more miles away in Ipswich.

Allowing my black stripes and dark coat to blend with the hazy smoke-ridden shadows of the few oil lamps they allow, I eventually find the poor, thin waif. I curl around her to warm her. In her sleep, she reaches out and cuddles me like a long-lost poppet. I allow her to restrain me, but remain weary and alert. I can't afford to fall asleep or relax.

The town of Ipswich has a Singer. One who knowing my shame, won't even nod her head at me, and in fact drives me from her town every chance she gets unless I am directly within the confines and surroundings of the jail. I am sure Jedidiah has told her of my shame in not Singing the child on.

How could I not have followed Bast's law? Very few of her children are born to Sing and I, as he said, profaned it. My lovely coat falls into disrepair and is tacky, even sickly looking. Once I caught a young hen from a nearby farmer, but was unable to bring it into the prison before the local Singer had divested me of it and sent me on my way with a strong bite to my shoulder for my troubles. I would sit and cry if I could, but that too would bring unwanted attention.

I am a pathetic sight indeed. I spend my resting time asking Bast how best to change my situation while not abandoning this poor child. Why must she suffer this way?

Dorothy has told the so-called investigators what they wanted to hear. Being only four how could she do anything but? Her mother gives birth in this filthy place to a lovely baby girl, but I believe Bast has given me a way to redemption, for I can see the miasma of death on this child which the mother has called Mercy. This is the first time since Dorothy, that I have seen the precursors of death. That night I Sing baby Mercy over to the other side. Her little soul, barely bright enough to be seen by me, gaily enters the small rift and pops out of existence. She was aptly named. For not only was her passing a mercy, but it has given me back my strength and clarity of mind and

I can see all the souls and their degrees of deterioration once again.

The child's mother is found guilty in the men's eyes and as summer wanes into late July, Sarah Goode is hanged for the crime of witchcraft. They tear the tearful and angry woman away from her sole remaining child. I suppose the only positive thing is they took the four condemned that day far away to a place called Gallows Hill in Salem town. This means that the child didn't have to hear the crowd and its taunts, nor see her mother swing from the rope.

Regardless of risk, I stayed with her this day and into the next. Little Dorothy has suffered much, and her mind is no longer her own. She eats dirt, talks in riddles, sings to herself, and dances oddly for no reason. The other prisoners, instead of taking sympathy on the child, have gradually become more and more afraid of her. I can see now the folly of my pity to leave a child walking this earth when their spirit is called onward. I will never again forsake my duty, but then too I am responsible for this waif and her condition. The bitter cold of another New England winter is coming quickly. I don't believe she has the ability to survive it. I have to find a way to get her out of this desolate jail. Her own father is unable to help her, although without his family, he has found work and lodgings a few towns over where they don't know quite all the gory details.

September wanes into October. And snow has begun to fall lightly, but it will soon blanket the town. I know my time is short. Searching out her father William, I find him sitting in the pub in Andover. This town too has had its share of witchcraft accountings and convictions. But none carry the name of Goode. And so William, Dorothy's father, has been left mostly in peace to find employment and lodgings. I follow him for a few days, staying hidden in shadows and alleyways; behind carts and under street debris. Eating is easy enough, as mice are rampant this time of year not quite ready to hole up, and venturing out during the warmest parts of the day. But I have given myself a new task. Now that I know where Dorothy's father can be found, I must try to find enough coin, specifically silver, to spirit away safely for William to redeem for his daughter's freedom. It's not as hard as it sounds, really.

Most housewives, hold back a coin or two from their family. I'm certain it's to be sure they always have the money when the tax man or church come calling, because one of the few hobbies in these little villages is drinking at the local pubs. Some are saving to bring more family over on the next wave of ships approved by the Great and General Court each year. And some just save out of a lifetime habit of saving. But the Parrish boxes are not generally locked, and sometimes a particularly sneaky and strong kitty can get her head in under the lid and lift it up, stealing as many as three coins in a single night. Running through the town with my shiny plunder however, is another matter entirely. I know I can't be discovered by the local Singer, and it is best that I not be seen by the other felines of the town either, lest they report my actions to her.

It takes an entire month to amass this large fortune. Hiding it has been incredibly difficult. I have had to hide it somewhere safe of course, where no cat, nor dog, nor pig was likely to find it and where no human would either. Finally, I settled on an old worn out and decidedly foul-smelling sock that had somehow been missed from someone's laundry.

To this, I have taken the sock and run with it through a pig's pen, a water trough, and a dog's excrement, ensuring that no creature coming haphazardly upon it would be likely to do more than make a wide berth. From there, I took the sock and stuffed it under a loose board that I had previously discovered in the Reverend Dane's own barn, making discovery very unlikely by anyone but a household member. It had the added distinction that, since most of the coins came from the church's own tithes, if it was discovered, it shouldn't be too terribly hard to get back!

December comes in like the proverbial lion with its snow and winds. I know now is the time if I am to ever free my young self-appointed charge from her Ipswich prison. I don't know how many coins I have stolen over the last months, but the old, smelly, sour sock is heavy. Heavier than I anticipated. The winds, snow and ice have made this task much greater than I anticipated. I can travel only a few paces before I have to set the foul bag in the snow on the ground and breath fresh air. Its weight is not something I am accustomed to, and the smell causes me to physically wretch. Another problem for which I had not taken into account, was the weight of the coins. The sock has stretched, and rather than carrying, I am closer to dragging this weight. After the fourth time of being forced to drop the bag to breathe, I hear the snow crunch behind me. It's late enough that I know no dogs are out and about, and the humans have all retreated to their warm homes.

I whip myself around, back arched, legs tensed, tail straight up in the air, with a low growl in the back of my throat. I have positioned myself over my ill-gotten gains, even though the smell has kept me from becoming aware of the imminent intruder.

Jedidiah strides up to me and stops.

"Give me your burden and let us be done with it," reaching under me to pick up the foul bag. He is taller than me, and doesn't appear to have the response to wretch at its smell as I do. I lay my fur down and relax my posture. After a brief moment of looking him in the eye, I turn around again and take off at a much faster pace to the homestead of the Faulkners, who had also become victims of the foul cries of witchcraft. The husband has fallen ill from convulsions, confusion and memory loss, and with his wife accused and imprisoned, he had been left alone in the home. His many children were unable to care for his failing body, and no willing caretaker since the stain of witchcraft was about. William had found refuge there in the form of work and lodgings.

We travel for several minutes passing through the town to the outer fence marking the Faulkner's home. Jedidiah stops, setting his burden down.

"Did you have a plan on how he is to discover his newfound wealth?"

"Not really," I reply. And in deed, I hadn't thought this far ahead. How was I to get into the home carrying this heavy object? How would I get past the children and ensure that only William be the finder?

Sighing heavily, Jedidiah grabs up the sack again, and with a quick dash and leap manages to jump straight up to the roof. He looks at me as if to chastise me further.

It takes me more effort. I have to find a route from the wood pile leaning against the house to an overhanging eave, and using claw and wing, lift myself up from there.

He waits stoically. Finally, we make our way to the chimney, and carefully work our way down it.

We have to be careful. For a fire, though banked at this late hour, is always lit. Still, the rough-hewn bricks give us adequate purchase. More than once I want to sneeze due to the black smoke rising up, but I restrain myself. I marvel at Jedidiah's strength and determination. His dexterity and agility are akin to that of a wildcat. No wonder he is the dominant tom in any place he chooses to be!

He glides into the room, and makes his way across to William's room. How he knew this was William's room I can only guess at. It is late, so no one is about. Dropping the stinking, wet, dragging sock-turned-money sack into one of William's shoes that he's placed at the foot of his bed, he turns and leads me back out of the room.

We find a place, hidden in the farthest rafter of the father's room and wait. The household dog doesn't even bestir himself to take notice of us. It's the first night in many that I have been warm and dry. We settle down together and sleep the rest of the night until the daybreak.

William wakes up to a particularly nasty odor that even his barn doesn't smell of. After relieving himself in the chamber pot, he begins a short search to find the offending smell. Lifting the still-wet sock sack from his shoe, he feels the weight of it and wonders first what it is, then how it got there.

However, most concerns are dashed when he finds a large handful of silver inside the offending item. Placing the coins under his pillow he quickly disposes of the smelly, now-empty sock in the fire while stoking it up. The children will be up shortly, and his duties to the family have to begin. His mind reels with how that much money could have found its way to him. Dressing quickly, he begins his day by getting the children up and set to their specified chores both inside and out, while his care of the father is his task.

The two cats slip out during one of the times that the children run back and forth, bringing water, emptying slop jars or chamber pots, and bringing in more wood to begin the break of fast meal.

It is December 10th, 1692, and young Dorothy has been in this horrible dirt and wood jail for almost nine months of her short life. But today her father William has come to, as some would say, "pay" for her release. Others would say, "bribe the local magistrate" for her release. But in the end, it really didn't matter, because the result was the same. Paying a ransom price of fifty silver pieces, he was finally able to buy the freedom of his only child.

Story 5

Peace's Foundling

The little black kitten leans way over the railing of the fast moving vessel. Theirs is a ship transporting needed goods from place to place. She enjoys watching the water slip by, as well as the new sights, sounds and scents. Stardust, her adopted mother, keeps a wary eye on her. It makes her nervous every time Mira does it. They are far out to sea and if she were to fall overboard that would be the end of her. Even though Stardust herself possesses wings, they aren't for flying and couldn't support her weight. Mira's wings are not yet fully feathered and would only help drag her down into the ocean's black depths. As much as the captain loves his pets, he would be of no aid, it's not as if they could stop the ship in mid-ocean to save one wayward kitten.

"For the hundredth time child, get away from the railing when we are at sea!" Stardust pleads with her adopted daughter. The little black kitten has, from the moment of her arrival, been a creature of great tenacity as well as mental strength. Unlike her own daughters, who were gentle and quick to follow instructions, little Mira questions everything and everyone. She tries talking to the crew, who merely laugh at her perceived antics. However, the end result is that the crew has fallen under her spell and would do anything for Mira. Stardust has always been the captain's pet and kept her distance and dignity from the crew. Not that they disliked her, it was just a matter of dignity and respect. However, being both a foundling and a vivacious baby, Mira knew each of the crew personally; their habits and who was most likely to give her what she wanted.

Unlike her adopted mother, Mira would snuggle up to any of the sailors offering comfort and affection and would be welcomed by all.

"Mother, you know I love watching the creatures of the ocean. Aren't they just marvelous?"

"Yes dear, they are. Now come over here please."

"But come see! The big whale is following us again. It's like she wants to talk to me!" Mira leans even further over the edge hanging onto the wooden banister by her claws. Stardust is practically in a tizzy watching her young child risk her very life to see a whale. Reenya leaps onto the railing and smacks the young Singer back with a soft paw.

"Stop being mean! She was trying to talk to me," Mira pouts. Reenya rolls her eyes while jumping gracefully to the wooden deck of the merchant ship they live on. But her task was accomplished. Young Mira has awkwardly climbed down backwards off the railing to the deck.

"Why can't I talk to the blue whale? She is huge–huge-er than this ship!" Mira's green eyes shined even in the bright midday light. Stardust walked up to her young charge and began washing her from ear tip to tail tip, to assuage her own nervous energy.

"We don't say huge-er dear. We say larger."

"Seela says I can say anything I want because I am just a common stray cat and not a real Singer," Mira pouts. Stardust stops her ministrations to hiss at her oldest daughter who heretofore had been laying with her eyes closed basking in the sunlight, her pretty, short tight-laying coat glistening in the moist air.

"Well Seela is rude and we won't listen to anything she has to tell you my dear." Stardust glares at her oldest daughter while returning to her tender ministrations.

Each day, Mira wakes up nestled safely at her mother's belly. Her morning consists of greeting the gentle captain and eating her breakfast served by the young cabin boy, Nathaniel. He's one of Mira's fans, and showers her with head rubs and lots of body pats. Some self-grooming becomes necessary after his tender ministrations, and Stardust helps her orphan child stay clean and sleek like a ship's cat should be. But the afternoons Mira spends on the deck, looking over the railing every day watching the huge blue whale who, it seems, has been following them–always keeping an eye on her. And in return, Mira tries communicating with it by meowing loudly over the splashing of the fast-moving ship in the deep waters.

The various shades of blue and gray have helped hide the large creature from the crew at first, but eventually, even they notice the sleek, eighty-foot sea creature following along. Its loud Song does not go unnoticed either. The deep tones rattle the bones of the ship on a subsonic level that the sailors all recognize. The crew enjoys this playful banter between kitten and whale, and even encourage it.

The night is quiet on a ship. The majority of men are sleeping, even the seas seem to calm down for some well-deserved rest. The only lights on the ship are from the topside lanterns, which cast yellow globes in short radiuses, leaving plenty of space for a furtive cat to find her way without being seen if she should choose to.

Stardust makes her way through the spaces of darkness, avoiding the puddles of light; on tufted paws, so no sound gives her away. She peers over the aft side of the vessel looking for the gray whale she knows is still within the area, and doesn't find her. Padding softly to the fore portion, there she can see a glint of silver off the water a ways away. Speaking softly so her yowls do not disturb the crew: "Waverider, we need to speak."

The water churns as the great creature makes its bulky way to the vessel's side. The whale turns on her side so that one of her full, deep eyes can see the minuscule by comparison cat.

"I need you to leave the foundling alone. Her head is already in the clouds, I don't need it to be in the ocean as well." The great whale remains silent. Her visible eye, not needing to blink like a land animal's, remains open and staring. Stardust is used to ruling both the animals and men she comes in contact with. Speaking with a Waverider is not what one does every day, and it has her feeling small and unsettled.

Breaking the awkward silence, "She is rare. She can see the Windriders. She can see the Waveriders. I wonder what else she can see."

The great gentle creature says softly, "It has been a long time since I have known such a one as her. The Windriders will soon be no more. And I fear we, the Waveriders, will go the same way. If we are lost, so too will be our stories, our Songs. Maybe it is good that she can speak to us all."

"It is dangerous and you know it!" Stardust hisses. "It is too much power for one alone; especially a foundling with no background or stories. I have had to give her my stories, and that is barely enough to satisfy her!" Her tone is both fearful and angry.

"How could the Goddess have left this little one to find her own way? It was believed that only once in every five centuries is such a one born–a Singer who can speak with others of the five elemental creatures: the Windriders, great dragons who soar the skies; the Waveriders, gray whales and blues who soar through the oceans; the Firestorms, who know no control or reason, who both cleanse and destroy; and finally, the Earthriders, who move mountains and cause the lands to shift. The once-born Singers share the old knowledge and languages and are said to be the only ones who in turn, can permit the elemental creatures themselves to pass on. It's a huge responsibility."

Stardust is exhausted by the duty she feels to Mira. But she is also scared for her.

"Teach her well, little Singer. She was given to you for a reason," the great whale intones, then rolls onto her belly, taking a deep breath and dives beneath the surface.

As the months go by, young Mira grows and blossoms. She becomes a beautiful and sleek cat, with shining eyes and coat; larger than her own mother had been, and larger than Stardust or her children. The crew and captain attribute her size to her endless appetite. At ports, the crew all boast about their mascot and many come to see her.

The day comes when Reenya is traded away to another ship's captain. Mira follows them to the new ship, skulking along the docks. The busy men mostly ignore her. The few that notice stop and goggle before continuing their tasks. She sees that Reenya is made much over, and petted and welcomed like a treasured object. And it is as it should be, she thinks. For who else can Sing these men's souls over, or talk to the creatures.

Turning away to return, Mira notices a grouping of three ships anchored away from the others. Her crew are furtive and deliberately trying to avoid the usual wares available to men coming on shore from sea. Curiosity peaked, Mira stops and watches for a short while. They stow away food stores, rum and water but her cargo holds remain closed and mysterious. Her mother is always telling her, she is too curious for her own good, but she can't seem to help it. After watching a while, she returns to her own ship to find her mother in absolute dread that they would sail without her. After roundly cuffing her, Stardust grabs her and begins grooming her head while purring more stories yet again for what must be the hundredth time.

A storm is coming. A big one and all the crew and those on land are nervous. Several ships leave in the hopes of skirting the destructive storm. Carrying tons of gold and silver coins, the Spanish ships stay very close to the coast line as is their custom, while the European ship that Stardust, Seela and Mira live on, venture further out from the shore into open waters. All were heavily laden.

As the winds pick up dramatically, the hurricane advances quickly and, one by one, the ships staying too close to the shores were sunk. All hands on board were lost. Maybe as many as a thousand men.

The whale's Songs can be heard throughout the waters, even over the sounds of the rampaging ocean, creaking timber of the ship, and the yells and calls of the men to keep the rigging in place and the ship afloat. Mira hummed a mimicry of the whale's Songs, finally understanding their meaning.

As the night wears on, the sailing ship is battered and bashed by the unforgiving ocean, but only a few lives are lost as they fall into the unforgiving waters.

At the breaking of the new day, the water has ceased its churning and the wind has returned to her normal pleasant breeze as if her anger or fury was spent. Only four men lost, and only one sail torn. Her cargo still safely ensconced below deck. Checking their position through their experienced chart master, they determine their course and set sail back to France.

The feline Singers relax a little, settling back into their usual routines. But Mira knew now what she was, more so than her mother could ever convey and what her purpose in life was to be.

Out in the waters, the Waveriders chase along with them for their journey; sharing their Songs with her, telling her their histories and tales.

Story 6

Seeing

"What on earth makes such an 'orrible sound?" Macky asks.

"It's just Ginger. She does that after every fight," George replies, knowing Macky knows this, as it's not the first time he's commented on it.

"It's called a battle," Peter chimes in, poking the fire more out of boredom than a need to keep it going.

"I don't care what it's called. It's just a bloody fight to stay alive and kill them Rebs," Macky proclaims a bit loudly. Laughter and sympathetic head nodding ensue.

The three men sit around the open fire doing those mundane things that must be done; darning clothes, cleaning weapons as well as plates and cups, while letting go of the day's earlier stress and tensions. At the next fire over, another small group of men laugh and pass around some homemade whiskey one of them has brought with him.

The smell of the fires, the sweaty horses and the sweaty mean all mix to make a unique and peculiar musk permeating the air. The cooling night atmosphere and the otherwise quiet surroundings lend a casualness that is not felt in the hotter light of day, when they must be on the lookout for enemy soldiers.

A fluffy orange and white tiger-striped cat comes strolling into the firelight's glow. Rubbing on each man in turn as she makes her way to the pot of thick stew that's simmering, and pieces of meat she knows await her. Seating herself next to the young corporal whose uniform jacket reflects his rank by the two chevrons on its sleeves, she reaches out and pats his leg. His companions smirk in amusement, while the young man reaches over and offers her a piece of the saved grouse.

"Ginger" is the name the young man gave her the first time he saw her. He was being trained to be a soldier, feeling sorry for himself being away from home; the farm and family for the first time in his life, when after a particularly hard day she had just somehow been there. Returning to his shelter tent, she was somehow just there on his cot. At first, he kept her presence from his tent mate for fear he'd be unhappy with her. But as time wore on, it became impossible to hide her. She became a company mascot of sorts, and was welcomed by most of the young recruits offering comfort and some semblance of normality in their rapidly changing world.

Young George always felt comfortable talking to Ginger, telling her his deepest secrets or just the daily chatter. She was a very good listener it turned out.

But here he was now. An Army corporal with duties and obligations that he never could have imagined. One of his tasks was during any battle, he was responsible for helping keep the men in line for firing; keeping them together. When a man fell, he was to keep the rest of them from straying and reform the line. Seemed almost obscene to him… *"Here, stand together and make a larger target for the enemy,"* but he was too well-trained, and at heart a good and honorable man, so he performed his duties the best he could.

So far Ginger had been there after every skirmish to sit with him and offer him what comfort she could.

Why she went onto every single battlefield afterwards and screamed such horrible sounds, he didn't understand or really much care. Only that she was there to be rubbed and petted and given the choicest bits of meats. No one, not even the captain complained about her noise. She offered comfort to anyone who asked it of her, after her self-appointed duties of, well… "screaming at the dead" were done.

Part of her self-appointed rounds was to visit all the campfires, checking in on all of the weary and heart-sick soldiers. It was amazing how these men who killed in the daylight would coo and coddle this lone feline. Moving on, she would wander through the hospital area checking on all the wounded, hopping on cots, sniffing, and seeming to give her approval or maybe her disdain. Who really knows with a cat after all.

Finally making her way to the captain's tent, he accepted her comfort and companionship gratefully, saving a bit of cheese for her; often enough that it was an open secret. Even the camp mutts that invariably follow all human groupings, seemed to take no notice her, never bothering her. Only one person in camp was not visited by Ginger. She kept herself apart from the young boy whose job it was to carry things, including the wounded, tools and other necessary items.

This young man Patrick, was himself fresh from Ireland. The oldest boy in his rather large family, who at the tender age of twelve had joined the Union Army to earn wages enough to send home. And although the Great Famine in his former country was over, it was still a struggle to survive. His father had come over early and established himself as a farmer and blacksmith, earning enough money to bring the rest of the family over in just a few short years. They had all been thrilled to not only make the journey, but integrate themselves into their new culture. But one of the things that had also come over to this new world with them, were their old superstitions and fears. And Patrick was quite sure the ginger cat who screamed on the battlefield was some kind of banshee from the old world, though he couldn't figure out how she had come to be here.

Days wore into weeks, and several small skirmishes were fought. Many men, on both sides of the war died. Ginger sang to them all, Union or Confederate. It didn't matter to her, only that their souls were given the release of peace and allowed to cross over to whatever came next. Men cycled through the company—some dying, some leaving for other regiments, companies, brigades or divisions.

All the men were treated to Ginger's particular kind of attention and affection, and very few refused her a good back scratch or chin rubbing. Those few hardened soldiers who couldn't see the value in such comfort and care, were left to their own devices. And still, Patrick watches her every night make her treks.

Time passed as it always does, even in war. A particularly fierce battle that had many dead, many more wounded, and in a densely-wooded area with hard-to-find footing or no daylight to peak through the trees' canopy, had soldiers shooting at most things that moved, and in some regrettable incidences their own men.

The call goes out to bring a stretcher, for the handsome captain has been hit by a musket ball in the thigh and is unable to remain on the battle ground any longer. He is bleeding profusely, even with as much pressure as he and the apron-clad medical assistant can apply to the wound. It must have nicked an artery. There is too much blood. The sounds of the shots continue causing a delay in the stretcher to arrive, which the captain can't afford.

The young Patrick and a new boy of a similar age, build and story called "Sean", race out onto the blood-soaked floor of the woodland. The shooting continues on around them, interspersed with the occasional boom from a 6-pounder field cannon someone has found a way to work into this engagement. Men screaming at irregular intervals make for a cacophony up-close, that Patrick and Sean wish they had never heard. Sean is shaking so much, he's unsure if he can hold the stretcher steady enough, but Patrick tells him to concentrate on his work and the lads are able to move the wounded officer to the back of the line.

Ginger is immediately on the stretcher at the captain's head, making little chirping noises. Both boys back away from the cot immediately adjacent in the tent, which hold a diminutive form lying covered with a bloody sheet. They exchange looks of horror. Rede the doctor, shoos the boys back out of the tent so he can attempt to save the young handsome captain.

At days end, when the fighting subsides and the camps have broken for the evening meals, there are still many dead on the forest floor. Ginger is about her regular self-appointed rounds, yowling softly at the dead on the field. She comes into camp in less than an hour's time, this instance coming up to the boys directly and sitting across from them. An almost ethereal figure, flickering with the firelight.

She stares at Patrick who refuses to look at her. Sean keeps nudging Patrick as if to gain courage from the other boy's attempts to dismiss the feline. Ginger blinks slowly, taking the time to delicately clean one of her paws from the ever-present dirt.

Patrick turns his body so as to not look at her sitting across the small, warm fire. Sean is caught between staring at her and watching Patrick. Finally, a young boy's curiosity gets the better of him and he lowers a hand out in front of him rubbing his thumb and fingers together while making a clicking noise with his mouth. Ginger stands up and stretches deeply before softly padding over to step into Sean's warm cross-legged lap. He scratches her behind her ears and rubs her from head to tail. A smile creeps onto his young face and his shoulders relax causing him to appear to shrink a bit. He doesn't really remember why he was afraid of this pretty little barn kitty. He does remember that they always had barn cats at home who would keep their farm free of rats and other predatory rodents.

Closing his eyes, he can see one of his barn cats and her babies playing in the hay and he remembers smiling; being happy and feeding them bits of bacon and fat from his mother's kitchen. Ginger rubs into his small chest, purring and rumbling as cats do.

Sean, still with his eyes closed, grabs hold of her burying his head in her soft shoulders crying. Crying to be here so far from home, to see so many dead, missing his mother and their small farm.

Patrick gets up, moving to another knot of men and fire, keeping a wary eye on the grieving pair.

Standing across from the gently licking flames is the handsome captain. His uniform clean and crisp, his face soft and gentle.

"I think it is time mistress," he whispers to the cat. She looks at him still purring and kneading within the young boy's grasp.

"Soon," she says gently.

The now well-dressed man calls to Sean, "Come boy, it's time for us to go". Sean snuffles loudly, looking up. The camp, usually noisy with men exchanging stories, dogs squabbling, pots and cups clanking; has become only so much background noise.

Looking at the captain, Sean stares with wide-eyed surprise.

Sean says, "But you died today. I saw it. I carried your body!"

"Maybe you should call me 'Michael' since you did indeed carry my body. But Sean, your friend

Patrick there, helped carry your body as well. And it's time to go now."

Wide-eyed with tears staining his face, Sean looks around. He realizes things are different. He can see the camp. He can hear the men, the horses, even the fire but he can't smell any of it. Sean realizes everything is muted as if through cloth or around a wall. He can make it all out, just not crisp or clear any longer, except for the captain ... errr ... Michael, and the fluffy ginger cat in his lap.

Sean absently continues to hold and pet the Singer who has placed her front feet on his knee and begun opening her wings. Michael steps through the fire coming to a stop in front of the pair. He bends down petting the Singer.

"Thank you for waiting for us."

The Singer nods her head slightly and gives him a slow blink showing her affection for the man.

Taking the young Sean's hand in his, he helps

him to stand one last time while Ginger hops to the ground delicately. "We are ready now," he says.

Extending her wings fully, Ginger Sings a quiet Song of peace and passing. The two figures fade slowly into the fire's smokey light.

The rest of the camp, except Patrick who has watched the whole scene in both fascination and horror, seem completely oblivious to the occurrence.

The small pop of the portal closing from within the flames goes unnoticed as just so much fire crackling. However, Patrick's wide eyes are glued to the scene that has played out in front of him. The Singer shakes her shoulders resettling her wings to where no one can see them, and walks straight to Patrick.

Placing her front paws on his crossed legs, Ginger tells him, "It's okay you know." She says, "A few humans who are part fae can see us. You needn't fear it, or us. In fact, many look upon it as a gift".

Patrick stares off for so long she begins to think he isn't processing her information.

"Okay," he finally says. Instinctively petting the fluffy orange and white-striped kitty, they settle in together like old friends.

Story 7

A Tale of the Sea

There was nothing special about my sister and me. Two small brown tabby cats with short coats, long tails and yellowish eyes. But we were welcome almost more than our human companion Joseph. Being ship's cats, we earned our keep by killing the vermin that are inherent to all such vessels – rats. We got the best treats and were almost of a protected status. But the humans didn't know our larger purpose because along with having rats, ships kill people. Injuries at sea not getting care, malnutrition on long voyages, dysentery, cholera and just the ordinary accident. People died. And when they died, they needed to have their newly-released souls led onto the next … well, whatever is next.

Ships without Singers–those few special winged felines whose power to croon an opening into the blanket of space and then either permit those happy souls to move on, or coerce those unwilling–those ships become haunted, and black and evil. When such a spirit is left to their own devices in this world, without the attachment to a body, it becomes a wicked nasty thing, capable of changing the very air around them into a blackness, drawing even the brightest soul's light from them. But Singers, those who can call forth the opening and permit and compel the souls to depart, are cherished.

We have long been ship's cats for centuries. And every ship needs its cats. But sometimes, ship's cats had to make these hard decisions. Even my grandmother is rumored to have gone down with her beloved owner and the ship. Ships so rarely sink these days. It's not like the old days, and I don't have a beloved owner, only Joseph. But he is kind and sweet, and he cares for us. He's taken my sister and me on several ships. Now we are on to another one.

It's mid-March and pouring. It is always humid and wet, but this is excessive even for Southampton. I am fat and heavy with babies soon to be born, and Joseph is feeding me all the best scraps and quite a few fresh cuts as well. I still bring about the demise of a few of the vermin from on the ship, but it's more a token really. I get winded easily and Polly, my sister, also a ship's cat, has taken over the majority of the hunting. She too is pregnant, but hers is a week or two earlier than my pregnancy. It's odd in today's world to have two Singers living so close together, but we were identical twins and inseparable.

We have been on this beautiful ship since its maiden voyage a few years ago and Joseph has always been tasked with taking care of us. He is a gentle soul, hailing originally from Ireland. He works in the kitchen where it's always warm. Polly prefers to be above decks, mingling with everyone.

I am a little more stoic than that, and enjoy laying about below decks. Our innate talents are rarely used onboard a ship like this. After all, it's not a pirate ship. Not many people die at sea these days, to need a Singer to see their soul over.

There has been a lot of excitement around the new ship arriving today and several of the staff will be transferring to her soon. Joseph is on the list of transfers as well, and I've heard him talking to the some of his friends about it.

Hugh in particular wants Jim to take both of us with him. He's never been particularly fond of us, but doesn't believe in tossing away the old superstitions. So therefore, all ships must have a ship's cat. But mostly, he is ignored. He is a good worker, but likes to drink a bit more than is good for him. Working in the boiler room means he has a lingering smell of smoke, char and metal.

March twenty-fifth comes along and I have given birth to three lovely sweet, fat babies. One is a Singer. Polly and I are overjoyed! She has taken over the duties of patrolling the lower decks, storage and even the engine rooms. The dirty, sooty, noisy engine rooms are always busy and it is hard to concentrate or even breath really, but they too must be kept vermin-free.

We were efficient, and all of the staff enjoy seeing us, including sharing bits of their meals. Most non-seafaring people think a cat is an unwelcome addition onboard a ship, but they'd be wrong.

Polly never complains, but she knows her time of giving birth is soon too, and we share a warm spot under Joseph's berth. He's given us an extra warm blanket and a few torn pieces of clothing to use to keep my babies safe and contained.

"'Tis not good to move wee babies like this," Joseph tells his mate. He's rolling up his few belongings into his duffle. His clothing, not the least of which to suffer the fate of being ignominiously stuffed without care for wrinkles or cleanliness.

"But there is naught to do my man. You got t' take one of them."

Polly returns from her rounds and slips under the bed to listen in, aware that this conversation is important.

"I know I know. I'll be takin' Jenny and her babies. It won't do to be movin' Polly at a time like this." And reaching down, Joseph picks up one of the sleeping babies in his large calloused worker's hand. He's gotten an apple crate from the kitchen and he places my baby in it gently on top of some only slightly soiled kitchen towels he's obviously nicked. But they are plush and soft and he places me in with them shortly.

We are cats, and so while we have said our goodbyes, we are not like dogs to whine and cry and make a fuss. "Stoic as a cat should be" a saying, even if it isn't.

Joseph throws his poorly packed duffle over his shoulder, as well as a smaller ditty bag holding his essential shaving equipment and soaps. Gently picking up the apple crate, we make our way together to our new ship.

A few short hours later we are installed in our newest room; me and the babies back under the berth. This ship is strikingly similar to our last. A few lavish details are different, such as a reception room before entering the dining room, the A deck's promenade is now enclosed in glass and steel, feeling more like a building than a ship. The generous use of carpeting in almost all of the upper-class areas is so soft on my paws. Of course, I had to go prowling about, learn my way around. Make sure of who was suitably impressed with me and who to avoid.

I learn that tomorrow's guests will begin arriving, and everyone and everything is getting last-minute instructions and polishing. Even the captain, a kindly older gentleman with a head of white hair, leans down to give me a full body rub and doesn't seem to mind the few loose hairs I leave on his trousers.

I return to my babies often, but still have a feeling that I need to see more of the ship. Once we are at sea, I am sure I will settle right down. The last ship I was on was so similar, I don't know why I can't seem to get my footing here.

Admittedly, the first-class passengers did seem to bring a lot more dogs onboard: nasty, dirty, yappy things. Below decks, there are cages of them, and more in the state rooms.

You'd have thought this was a kennel not a luxury ship. It's a wonder anyone can sleep! I've never minded dogs before, but things are irritating me more than usual. It's most likely just that this is the first time I have ever not had my sister with me. We were each other's confidants and helpers and I miss her terribly. Crooning to my babies, sharing the Song of our kind with them settles me a little bit, enough to get some sleep. A single wing covers my brood, protectively reminiscent of a mother bird protecting her nest. Something very unusual as anyone could look down and see us.

Our first full day at sea, and we have stopped at Cherbourg France to pick up a few more passengers. We are late due to a disturbance during our departure.

The evening wind is subtle and lovely but I don't stop to enjoy it, I continue my journey through the ship, seeking whatever it is that is disturbing me. Our early departure has left me more unsettled than ever.

It is very rare, but we almost came into contact with another vessel in the narrow channel due to so many ore ships being moored. Some kind of labor strike I heard tell of, but very scary. I could have leapt the distance between our two ships!

My unease has grown to restlessness. During this brief stopover, I have even moved my babies into the captain's quarters instead of the below decks. I feel a bit better in here. There is more space. It's much cleaner, and the kindly captain even held the door for me two times to bring my babies in, so clearly he is not against my move. As I've said earlier, ship's cats are always welcome.

But this morning we sail for Queenstown in Ireland, Joseph's home and mine. My mind is made up: I am taking my children off this vessel the very moment we dock. There is only a two-hour window, and I have to pick up and bring my children to

Joseph's house. There, I know his wife will care for them and I will call out to other Singers to come care for my special little one. I have to bring my babies off this ship.

From the protected view railing of the crew's promenade, Violet can smell the sea and get her last few minutes of peace before her passengers arrive and are ensconced in their cabins. As she is watching the docks and all of the humanity bubbling both into and off of the ship, a quick movement of a cat carrying its kitten, along the runway, down the ship and onto the bench, catches her eye. The little cat is running as fast as she can without dropping her precious cargo. She is so quick, and seems to be almost flying with speed. After having watched this twice she looks over to the gentleman next to her, blinking in surprise.

"Why would Jenny be taking her babies off the boat? "Well, that's bloody odd," Violet murmurs.

"What's odd lass?" asks the man. He's clearly a

bit taken aback by her language, but she couldn't help herself. The ship's cat just jumped ship, ... or at least that's what it *appears* to be! Violet relays what she had just seen, and he snorts in bemusement.

"It's a cat. They do as they please. Didn't she just leave Joseph's berth for the captain's? Probably as fickle as any woman, and found somewhere else that better suits her."

He puts out his cigarette giving her a look that clearly says she's a foolish woman, and heads back inside to his duties.

"Ship's cats don't just leave them!" Violet rushes off to find Joseph, no small task on a ship this size. Passing the captain's quarters, she sees Joseph stepping out of them looking perplexed himself.

She grabs a hold of his sleeve as she relates the tale of having watched the ship's cat take two of her babies off and into the town. About this time, Jenny pushes past both of them and into the captain's cabin, once again at a mad dash. She grips her last baby who squeaks out in surprise at being awakened so brusquely.

"Come now puss, what's the matter," Joseph calls to Jenny. But she is in a hurry, and leaps past both the people, not even glancing at them or so much as looking their way. Joseph and Violet follow her path back to the runway, and once again down the ship and onto the benching below; then through the busy and cluttered aisles and streets, until she disappears down an alleyway.

A new junior mess hall steward comes up to Violet, "Hey there, you best be going, your guests is a callin' for ya." Violet motions the youngster away, still staring down at the docks.

"And you ... you ain't allowed to be up here. You need to get off this side of the boat and go below where you belong," he says indicating for Joseph to leave the promenade.

Violet turns to him, "Mind your own business and have some manners before I box your ears, you child!" Her face is red with concern and distress over watching the ship's cat abandon the vessel. Joseph is clearly unnerved.

"Me wife is only a few blocks down that lane, Jenny

knows this. She was born there. I bet that's where she's going." He pauses mulling this development over.

"Well, if she says to get off the ship, who am I to say naught?" He turns, brushing past the rude young steward who huffs off, angry at being dismissed so out-of-hand. Violet watches them both go, lost in thought. Should she stay?

Without a ship's cat, that was a bad omen. But she had an amazing position–one she couldn't easily replace, and certainly not if she voluntarily gave this one up. Telling herself she was being a superstitious fool, she turns to go below decks to assist her passengers as she was employed to do; putting the odd situation of Jenny and her kittens out of her mind so she can fully concentrate on the needs of her charges without disruption or discord.

Joseph however, has a different view of things. He finds himself breaking out into a sweat at the loss of what he considers his ship's cat. He has cared for her and her sister since they were born and even though a lowly scullion, he was afforded certain advantages being the de facto owner and caretaker of Jenny. But that aside, he is scared.

Why would she have taken her kittens off the ship? Where did she take them to? He no longer had enough time before the ship left port to go home and ask his wife if Jenny and her kittens were there, even running it was too great a distance to get there, get his answers and return to the vessel.

His family really needed him to have this job. White Star lines paid well compared to some others, and if he left now, he wasn't sure he could get back on. Now, he wished he had brought Polly with them. Then there would still be a ship's cat ... or maybe she would have fled too! What if they knew something he didn't? Well, who was he to ignore the obvious. He could find other work. Making up his mind finally as he reached his berth, he once again rolled up his meager belongings into his duffel along with his still-packed ditty bag. Retrieving the apple box and towels he had used to bring Jenny here, he headed home, hoping his dear wife would understand his reasoning, confident that Jenny and her babies were already safely ensconced back at his home.

But Jenny hadn't left the ship! Not for good, in any case. Yes, she had sprinted using her wings to give her lift and speed, carrying her babies one at a time to the kindly wife of Joseph.

Sarah was home tending the kitchen, when Jenny dashed in through the window and virtually dropped her first kitten at her feet–her sacred Singer kitten. She paused just long enough to be sure Sarah had not only seen the baby, but was kindly disposed to care for it in the softening of her expression and sudden crooning while picking it up. Satisfied, Jenny races back to bring the second baby, and then shortly thereafter her third and final precious baby. But in truth, it the Singer-gifted baby she was most worried about.

Allowing herself a brief taste of the cream from the milk jug kept on top of the small ice box the family had received as a luxurious present early in their married life, she briefly rubs on Sarah's skirt before leaving her for the final time. Knowing she will never see this, her home and her children again.

Joseph arrives with his bags about a half an hour later, inquiring about Jenny and her kittens. Sarah tells her what she knows of the story, and together they understand what Jenny herself already understood. That ship was doomed.

Seventy-two hours later, the grand luxury passenger liner continues to steam her way across the Atlantic Ocean towards New York. During the last three days Jenny has not caught a single rodent, but instead had been poking her nose into every single lifeboat, checking out its hull both above and below, and in general trying not to be overcome with grief and fear. She knew what was about to come, and with certainty many would die. Jenny had come across death before being a Singer. It was what she was born to do. But on this scale, she didn't know if she had it in her. Jenny would slink by the now-full kennels below decks knowing what their fate was;

knowing that she couldn't help them. But what really sent her into fits of despondency were seeing the passengers' children. Knowing that most would not survive. The very ship itself had taken on a pallor of sorrow and woe attached to it, as if fate herself knew and grieved.

It was on the tail end of this third day that the unthinkable happens. The ship grazes an iceberg. If you were on one of the several promenades, you would barely feel it. A simple shudder and you would wonder what it was. But if you were below, far below, in the bowels of the ship ... you knew. You knew this wasn't good.

It was 11:40 pm, and enough damage was done, that this ship of dreams was going to sink. Jenny placed herself in the upper-most promenade and began her Song. No one cared. No one heard. But she sang, for all her strength and ability she sang and at first, slowly a wandering soul would be drawn to her Song and then permitted and encouraged to travel on to what comes next. Soon though, the ship starts tipping, raising its tail in the air like a dog bowing. Jenny has to grip that fine carpet with her claws to maintain her balance and start sidestepping loose debris that comes rolling her way. And still she Sings. The ship tips further and large pieces of furniture are displaced but that lovely carpet gives her purchase, keeping her upright as well as using her wings for balance. Never has she ever thought about how she would accomplish this Herculean task as the more and more souls come. The cracking of the metal hull warns her that things are about to change, and she flies to a higher vantage point.

During her brief discontinuance of the Song, the souls still follow her, knowing hers is the only respite, the only chance to leave this ship, even though their bodies are done.

When the ship can finally stand no more weight, she cracks in two like some demented kitchen chef cracking an egg. The larger aft portion of the ship rapidly disappears into the inky blackness of the frigid water while the screams of the still-living, clinging onto the remaining piece pierce the night. The stern portion remains, bobbing like a top.

Now there are hundreds of souls clamoring around her for surcease. Their bodies already having released them, they flee still in abject terror. Jenny's Song continues but there is only so much a single Singer can do, especially under these circumstances.

The opening Jenny can create with her Song is only so big, and no more than a few souls can push their desperate way through. Just as in life they pushed to get above deck to a life boat, their souls now push and shove and fly around trying to fit into the rift that was only meant for a few. A desperate crewman hanging on, hears what he thinks is howling from the lone ship's kitty, and in a fit of desire to save her makes his way over to her, gripping her in his strong hands, not seeing the streaking spirits or noticing her wings. He was once a kind man, and as such he tries to throw her far down below towards a lifeboat he can see, hoping he can at least save the poor screaming cat. As she is flung from the rapidly sinking remains of the aft piece, Jenny has to stop her Singing to right herself, exposing her wings and attempting to softly land somehow, somewhere. But there is no place other than the icy water. The life boats are too far away, and as the final piece of the tail of the ship gets sucked below, it creates a vortex of undertow. Jenny's wings aren't made for flying. She's not a bird after all, and even some birds can't fly! Jenny's wings only allow her to get caught up in the powerful suction made by the final disappearance of the entire aft section into the water.

Water much too cold for her, or indeed any warm-blooded creature to survive for very long. The still-remaining souls follow her into the water in hopes she will again Sing. But her Song is done. Her wings tangle together in the too-strong current, and the shock of the bitter twenty-eight-degree water steals her breath, rendering her unconscious.

Whether she died of hypothermia or because she never again raised her head from the water doesn't really matter. Eventually the remaining souls began to scatter, realizing their hope for going on to the next existence was gone.

The little floating body of the cat is not noticed by the poor cold and wet traumatized survivors, bobbing in the dark in their tiny powerless wooden life boats. It doesn't matter that you can see her wings any more. She watches her lifeless body from above, her own little soul flitting about desperately unhappy being unable to have completed her task.

It is the darkest and coldest time of the night, that time after midnight before the sun even thinks about rising over the horizon. The ship Carpathia has responded to the distress call sent out and begins rescuing the few remaining passengers still floating in the icy ocean.

As the sun rises around 5:20 and the rescue continues, there are bodies readily seen floating in the water, making the already grisly task grimmer. It is around 8:50 in the morning following the sinking of the Titanic, that the Carpatia takes all of the living survivors and turns heading for her New York destination.

Story 8

Duty

Stop … stop right there ... advance no further. Stop, I said, stop. Stop. Stop!"

The diminutive cat halts her advance towards the debris and wreckage. It's already hot out, even for 9 am. But that's the desert for you. Dirty, dry, hot, bleak and little cover. The feline sits down in the dusty grime.

"I have a job to do. These people are deceased and I must Sing their souls over to the other side." The Singer tries to reason with the aggressive barking dog.

"Mine … mine to protect … leave us alone. Mine. They are mine, must protect."

The cat purses her lips, which for a cat is rather difficult. Her tail begins to twitch but just at the very tip displaying her aggravation.

"I need you to calm down my friend. How about using full sentences? And they are dead. They are beyond your help. It is my turn to help them."

"No. Bad Cat. Go away. Mine, mine to protect." The dog has worked herself up into a virtual frenzy. The day is getting warmer and the little Singer would much rather be inside her cool home where there is a big fountain, lots of tiled flooring and air conditioning, unlike most of the mud huts the vast majority of the population live in. But she too, like the excitable dog in front of her, knows her duty. And that is to Sing these five, no make that six, souls onto the next realm. Whatever that may be.

The sixth soul is that of a young child. It is smaller than the others, dimmer, somehow less vibrant. She almost missed it with all of the noise the dog is making and the five vibrant shimmering balls of energy flitting here and there. The dog is catching each ball as it tries to leave the general area. Some pre-programmed space or distance that the dog perceives is in her scope of containment. It's actually very helpful really, as then the Singer could keep her Song soft and gentle, rather than forceful and pushing. It is always better to open the rifts when the souls are nearby, and allow them to find their own way in. If Singers have to open rifts and call the souls, it is much more traumatic for the soul and takes so much more energy from the Singer.

A Singer can collapse, virtually unconscious for days after a particularly difficult task. And that is dangerous in this world, so much more so because the humans that populate it no longer believe in the existence of magic, or of the extraordinary. And seeing a cat collapsed by the roadside with wings outspread would be disastrous. It could change the whole human-Singer relationship. She really didn't consider herself magical, just tasked with the out-of-the-ordinary. She wished the dog would get out of the way and stop making so much noise.

"Why don't you tell me what happened to them?" She asks, hoping it will distract the dog.

"Sure, yes, of course. Hey ... mmpphf!" The dog had to go retrieve one of her charges, catching the ball of glittering shimmering light in her mouth and bringing it back to the unseen perception of what was considered, in her canine mind, not too far away.

"We were coming to meet up with another unit. One that has Casey in it. He's a lieutenant who always has good things to eat in his pocket. He will share if I ask nicely, but we have to play this game first. He pretends like he ignores me but I can feel his body tense up. And I jump on him, in the front and sniff the pocket, then he will smile not showing his teeth, and open it up ... the pocket that is, not the mouth. And let me see it before he gives it to me."

"My partner J'nab, that's short for Jonathan McNab ... he's who trained me and takes care of me. He smells of soap and tooth paste, he carries the hair of a small baby person and whom I am to listen to because he is the boss who can take my dinner away and put the muzzle on me. But he doesn't do those things, he lets me go to the end of the leash to sniff the bad things and find them…"

She pauses in her run-on dissertation of the people she is familiar with, and her interpretations of their interactions. A sorrowful sound fills the air, one of great despair and sorrow. Her mouth forms the howl of utter desolation and the sound causes the cat to flick her ears back in annoyance.

"Stop that Dog, you will bring all of the enemy down upon us!". Glancing from side to side, the Singer twitches her entire tail in annoyance and slight fearful concern. It would not be good to be caught out in the open like this. It's daylight and while she is a small creature whose brown and rust coat manages to blend in with the dirt and rubble, it wouldn't protect her from being seen.

"Bring the enemy, I will kill them all! They have killed my masters and mates. They have harmed that which I am to protect!"

The cat rolls her eyes at this and gives a sneeze of further annoyance. For cats, whether they are

Singers or not, don't see the need to protect anyone who is not them or their kittens. It's part of what has kept them secret, safe and mysterious. The dog pauses and looks around as if lost. The rapidly warming day is causing the bodies to start to smell. Flies have found the bodies as well.

"That one is Lance Corporal Jared. He just came to us. He was only ours to protect for a short while. I think he was a little afraid of me. No, not afraid ... intimidated. And that one over there, he just had a baby they say, but I can't smell it on him. He was crying the other night talking on the electronic machine to his mate, she's called his wife I think. His wife always sends him stuff to give to the local children, and they all pet me. I don't think they are supposed to do that, but I like it and so does J'nab. I like the children. They are nice to me."

The dog stops, cocking its head. The heat is beginning to give shimmer to the desert in waves. A heavy sigh is released.

"I didn't know this child. He smells different than the local children. He came from behind the vehicle. He is not older or dressed differently, but he does not smell of the dirt and spice the local children do. This child is clean and his shoes are better-made."

How the canine can tell this the Singer doesn't know, but she is sure that none-the-less, it is true. The cat brings her wings out in anticipation of being able to complete her task of seeing these souls over to whatever comes next. The dog continues on, still guarding her self-appointed charges.

"I should have seen him, heard him, smelled him. I would have smelled the explosives or metal. But I was out front. I caught the movement from the side of the vehicle and came running over. It was too late. I am a bad, bad dog. My Sergeant J'nab had told me to 'seek' at the front of the vehicle. I wasn't looking to the side. Why wasn't I looking to the side? But that's not how we trained in Kandahar Airfield. I was doing what I was trained to do, what was asked of me. It should have been enough. Why Cat? Why wasn't it enough?"

A tiny cloud spire of dust can be seen off in the distance. No telling how far it really is. The Singer can't hear anything, so it's got to be far enough away to still have time.

"Dog, I have to Sing. I have to let them travel on. Their souls can't stay here. As you did your job, let me do mine."

"Even the child's I suppose?" The tired canine looks at her balls of flittering lights.

"It's not fair you know. They use children that way. Teaching them to kill us with their homemade bombs. That's why we have to be careful. I didn't know this child. Be sure he crosses over too, won't you Cat? It's not his fault. Children should never be used as a tool of war."

Bobbing her head in affirmation she replies, "Of course, Dog. All the souls. And yours too. It is time for you to let go of your body and come away as well." The Singer places her delicate cat's paw on the Belgian Malinois' gore-covered muzzle. How this animal can still be alive she thinks, is a testament to the Military Working Dog's grit and determination to protect her charges to their last breath. There is more of the poor creature on the outside than the inside and the flies have been as merciless as if she were already a corpse. The dust plume has become slowly more defined and larger; now the Singer can hear the motors of the oncoming convoy. She Sings her gentle Song to the gathered souls, allowing them to quickly and safely pass over into the next realm. It takes only a few brief moments and they are gone.

The intensity of the dog's gaze is gone, her voice is feint, fragile even.

"I am tired ..." The military canine breathes out softly for the last time.

Bowing her head in respect, the Singer give a small push of her energy to the new shimmering mass that is the valiant dog's soul, to pass through the rift created with the Song, to be sure the great defender's spirit moves on peacefully.

The military convoy rolls up to the burnt-out shell of the Humvee and the remains of its former occupants. Lieutenant Casey steps out of his patrol's vehicle to assess the remains. He knows this group of soldiers. They were his friends, his comrades. And the MWD too. Her name was Suzie. She liked to jump on him like an untrained pup checking his jacket pockets for the treats his wife would bake at home and send.

Story 9

A Murder of Crows

"Murder ... Murder ... Murder ... Murder ... Murder ... Murder ... Murder ..." the raven shouts from the tallest branch in the nearest tree, looking down upon the little body of the dead Singer. Several others of his brethren take up the call shortly making for a cacophony of noise; no one for a good mile is sure to miss. All of the local animals stop their morning routines to listen. The ravens will cry for any number of reasons, but to set up a din in the cry of murder is not usual in this little town. The younger birds–those without mates, glide down to the body of the cat and begin the task of covering it. This is not a carrion feed, but rather a sacred duty given to them from the gods themselves. As the cousin to Bast, Horus was tasked with seeing the souls safely to her by protecting her children in their task to Sing the souls to her. But Horus and Set were so busy fighting one another for dominance, that Horus delegated this task to the lesser raven. And ever since, the raven has taken his task very seriously. Only those birds with babes in the nest were exempt from their duties, and then only for a short time.

Today, a young fox had come across the body of a house-sized cat and had thought, "Aha! Today is my lucky day for I shall eat without hunting!" But upon picking up the body to take back to her den to eat in peace, the Singer's great wings had fallen open to cover the fox's nose and face. So startled was the fox, that she dropped the cat's body, yipped, and even jumped into the air, fearful of some deceit or danger. Her red fur quivering and bristling, her nose twitching until she realized what it was that she had found. Then, she sank to the ground, her belly scraping the dirt and she lifted her muzzle and let loose with a series of short staccato, but high-pitched wails. This is what drew the small flock of unmated ravens to the area initially. From there, they set up the cry of murder ... attracting more ravens, and others as well.

Several local house cats came by to see what the ruckus was about, but took off quickly after seeing the Singer's remains. The fox's mate came to see what she was so upset about and then stayed to comfort her. An owl took up a branch in the tree that the ravens occupied. He kept a wide-eyed watch of the proceedings, making sure all was as it should be. For although the little Singer's body had died, her soul was still flitting around, unsure why she hadn't passed on. The ravens continued their wide-mouthed cawing in the cry of murder for hours, while two mated pairs, older and wiser than the flock of bachelors, took over the arduous task of finding enough loose twigs and plant debris to cover the body including the wings.

TAILS OF THE SINGERS

As the night comes on, many animals both wild and domesticated, come by to pay their respects, to mourn, to grieve and to worry about how to bring another Singer to the area. The ravens are finally quiet as true night falls. The body has been sufficiently hidden so that any predator, not of the old beliefs, will disturb the remains. Bears, badgers and their ilk will not find the sacred cat.

The bright ball of iridescent soul still flits near the owl, awaiting its time to travel. With the fullness of night, the owl gathers its charge and flies on to where it knows of another Singer in another county in a town of man. He flies through the darkness unhampered by either the weight of the task, or the soul itself. The collection of ravens follows him in silence, acting as both guard and escort.

The town below comes into view, lit to look alive from above, with its pollution of artificial electric suns. But the owl knows where he is going and continues on towards a small darker spot that is an ancient cemetery in this outlaying town.

Its iron gate is permanently open, although it is no longer accepting new residents. It was long ago filled with those who had passed on and been immortalized by their loved ones. The owl settles himself upon a large old stone Celtic cross, and releases the little ball of energy. The crows settle nearby and begin their cawing again, only this time it is a call for the local Singer to come.

A rustle from the side, and the local Singer has arrived ... her wings extended to lend her lift and speed, though her body is too heavy for genuine flight, in her haste to respond to the ravens' demands. She comes forward to face the owl and gives a short bow while resettling her wings of silver and white. In the night's artificial light from a town not quite out of reach, she seems more ethereal than normal. The silvered coat glowing, her green eyes gleaming. Following behind her is a young kit, also a Singer but clearly not old enough to travel alone or perform the duties given to them by the Goddess yet. And though not afraid, this kitten is wary, having never seen her mother called in such a manner, nor her responding with such haste.

They listen to the ravens' cries and to the owl's calmer story. Bowing her head, the maternal Singer spreads her wings and begins her gentle song. The other creatures settle into a reverent stillness and soon the little spirit whisks itself away joyfully into the next world. The rift closes with a soft pop and the conclusion of the Song. The night resumes its usual tenor.

"What happened?" asks the attendant Singer. The ravens begin their cry of murder shattering the night's calm. Owl flutters his wings and hoots for silence and calm.

"We do not know, blessed one. A young fox found the body, thinking it an easy meal. Then sent out the call once she became aware of who she had stumbled upon."

The Singer looks to them then replies, "Call upon the fox again, for none of us can smell what she and her mate can. Ask her to discover all her nose will tell her and to report back. That Singer was young, and I see no obvious reason why she should be dead so soon."

The ravens shuffle their feet uncomfortably and bob their heads in agreement and the need to do something.

"We shall all meet here again in three-day's time. If there is foulness afoot, we must needs know."

All the gathered assembly disperse to accomplish the Singer's task.

Once the graveyard is clear, the daughter Singer steps forward.

"Mother, what happened? Why did that other Singer die? Was she really murdered?"

"I don't know my child, but whatever happened we shall add her life's ending to our Song from this point forward."

They take their leave of the old cemetery. This isn't their usual place of residence, but they do tend to come here a few times a month as the local population for some reason has taken to bringing their recently deceased pets to the old graveyard. And almost invariably those souls need to be helped into the next. Most creatures no longer have Singers of their own, and rely on those that do. Dolphins and whales are almost entirely born able to Sing. So are alligators and crocodiles, but they are so surly most natural creatures avoid them. Only the followers of Bast generally dare to take on the larger ones. Therefore, this Singer and her daughter have included in their territory this portion of the humans' domains.

Three days pass quickly, and as night falls all the concerned creatures, as well as those tasked with finding answers, show up gathering again before the large Celtic cross awaiting the arrival of the silver Singer with the green eyes and her daughter. Night comes on, and a quiet murmuring of the crowd partially masks the arrival of the soft-footed padding from the Singers. Their sudden appearance sitting on the outstretched arms of the cross lend an air of royalty to the proceedings.

The wise owl takes a step forward, moving awkwardly on the ground. He dips his head once to signal the start of the proceedings. The young red fox bitch steps out timidly from behind him, and looks up at the Singers.

"Sacred ones. I found the cause of the other Singer's death," her voice is quiet but sure. "It was one of the poisonous serpents of this land. I was able to follow it for a short while, but its scent went into its burrow and I dared not follow any more." Her pause causes all the others to shift and shuffle a bit.

Jaylen the silver Singer looks around the group, giving her a moment to think.

"Raven clan, would you be so kind as to somehow convince a descendant of Horus, the great Falcon, to come treatise with me?"

Looking at the owl and the red fox, Jaylen tells them, "You have done well, and I thank you. Your tasks are complete." By way of dismissal, Jaylen shifts her position on the stone arm of the cross so as to be looking up at the ravens in the tree.

"Find a falcon who descends of Horus and ask him to meet here. Old graveyards are neutral territory for the likes of us. Find me when you do, and thank you." The group disperses, leaving only Jaylen and her daughter Rayla.

"Why mother?"

"Why what daughter?"

"Why ask for a descendant of Horus? What can a hawk do? "

"Watch and learn little one. Though we are all descendants of the great gods, many have forgotten their assigned tasks. Some need only be reminded; some are so lost as to be forgotten, and others are no longer sure of their own heritage."

The ravens try for days to find a falcon in this modern land who acknowledges the ancient heritage. Some chase the birds and attempt to pull them out of the sky with claw and beak. Others who have no mates, flee under the hoard that the ravens have become in carrying out the Singer's instructions. Even the humans of the land begin to notice something strange going on, as a pack of ravens travels, seeming to bully and attack lone hawks.

Finally, the ravens find an old hawk sitting alone on a high-tension wire, watching them as they continue their search. The hawk tilts his head as the bulk of the murder of crows alights onto the tension wires, while others soar on the drafts to keep afloat.

Ravens are direct creatures with no room for subterfuge. Part of their difficulty in convincing a falcon is that not one takes the lead, but they all speak at once. It is very overwhelming to solitary animals such as falcons and hawks.

This one seems to be less bothered by their noise than most. When the raucous noise dies down, finally the large hawk looks over and picks one bird among the flock to address.

"Your task would have been easier had you actually known the difference between a hawk and a falcon, little ones. But I have heard of your search."

Feet shuffle and re-grip the wires. The ones

flying above swoop and dive but remain silent.

"Why is it you seek one of the old blood?" And again, the group begins its loud cacophony of information ...

"We search for a falcon for the Singer."

"A Singer needs help."

"The Singer commands it."

"The death must be avenged."

"Apep is evil."

It seems as if each bird individually has a piece of the tale, and no one bird has the all of it. But together, the hawk is able to parse out what they want and he thinks to himself, "Why not?"

Rustling his great wings, he calls out, "Enough!" Silence falls again; several of the smaller younger ravens nervously take flight to resettle further away on the line.

"Show me where your Singer is," the old hawk commands. The large group of birds takes flight heading back to the little silver Singer's graveyard. The hawk follows silently at a much higher altitude using far less energy and drawing much less human attention.

Jaylen and Rayla are awaiting the arrival of the hawk, when the group finally alights in the graveyard.

"Welcome Hawk – I am Jaylen and this is my daughter Rayla. We seek your help. A sister of ours was killed by a serpent, a descendant of Apep. We ask that you, as descendant of Horus, God of Secret Wisdoms, Truth, and the Avenger, to extract that vengeance for our lost sister."

Using one outstretched wing, Jaylen uses it in a bowing motion as she inclines her head to show deference to the elder creature. Rayla, seeing this, follows suit in her awkward kitten way, her wing not quite ready to respond to her commands, brushes the ground, disturbing the dirt. She takes a step back using the space to reel in her wayward appendage. Her whiskers smooth back in frustration at her lack of coordination.

Inclining his head, the hawk introduces himself as Amr ... "I find it amazing that in this, the age of man and technology, there are those who still believe and follow the ancient ways. Gods have not walked the earth in longer than a trimillennium. What makes you think I care? Either about your cause or a dead cat? You know I would eat such prey should I happen upon it."

Rayla begins to stand up her fur raised, her back arched. The ravens above shuffle their feet, flap their wings and bob their heads in fear and anticipation. Jaylen looks at her daughter sternly to settle herself but only blinks a slow leisurely blink at the insolent tone of the hawk.

"Are you through being uncouth and foul-mouthed Amr? Or do you truly need a history lesson at your advanced age? As a descendant of Horus, you may ask his permission to use the seeing eye to see the past event or the future one. And as such, know that a child of Bast was murdered by a child of Apep."

Amr sighs heavily clacking his beak in frustration. Never had he encountered in his long life such devotion to an ancient and dead religion.

The silence stretches out. Amr's head is looking back and forth assessing the situation. At his age, she was right, he didn't have much longer to live. Already his eyesight was not what it once was, his bones hurt and he missed more meals than he caught.

Coming to a decision, Amr dips his head in a bow and proclaims, "I shall do as you ask little sister. But upon one condition ..." Jaylen inclines her head, her deep green eyes fixed on the large bird.

"When I die, you shall Sing me over as well. For without being sent over, our spirits remain here to become so much whispering winds".

"I would have done so anyway, had I a way to know when you left your body. You need not have bargained that away, but I accept your terms. Please find the young red fox the ravens will lead you to, to learn the location and identity of the vile serpent."

The large hawk launches itself into the sky giving a piercing cry. The ravens all follow him with their louder din overwhelming the single sharp shriek.

Trailing the noisy flock of birds once again they quickly find the red fox's den with her family. The hunt for the serpent is on. Using her keen nose and memory for scents, she retraces her steps to the burrow she previously found. Nosing around brings the sharp reptile's odor into immediate relief. The fox yips and hops on her front feet once to indicate the burrow is indeed occupied. Knowing the serpent won't come out willingly she begins digging at the entrance to enlarge it.

One of the younger smaller ravens dives deep in the burrow to peck at and harry the snake to rise to the surface. Backing out of the den in haste, he narrowly avoids being bitten as the serpent strikes at him. Coming up to the top, the vixen backs off, still yipping to distract the snake. The ravens all settle in to nearby fences and bushes to watch while the hawk circles lower. Beset on all sides, the snake coils itself ready to strike any who get too near. Like a silent deadly freight train, the hawk dives straight down from out of the sky, after the snake. The ravens caw louder, and flap about to draw its attention. The hawk makes a devastating strike in the middle of the snake's back, picking it up with his sharp talons.

Unfortunately, enough of the head is left free to turn and bite the great bird and he drops him back to earth. Even with a broken and bleeding back, the snake is still lethal to the small animals attempting to end it. Jaylen steps in front of the assembled animals having appeared out of nowhere and silence falls.

"Why? Why did you kill one of our kind? It makes no sense unless we were hunting you."

The snake is now panting, its body quivering with the struggle to stay coiled.

"Because I could. What other reason can there be? We are older than time, older than Ra. We were here when the world was new and Ra was sent here."

Jaylen is saddened and angry that this descendant of the gods has chosen this path. She gathers herself up to deliver the final strike to the dying serpent.

"I don't think I shall Sing you on." Before she can strike, a blur of motion from her side causes her to hesitate. The streak of gold-brown fur races by her, grabs the snake in its canine teeth both crushing it and snapping his own head up to swallow it in the same motion. Turning to face the gathered ensemble, the large coyote holds its head to the side, tongue lolling out, eyes laughing.

Everyone in attendance is so startled they have frozen in place. Bowing down on his front legs, the coyote's yellow eyes are on a level to meet Jaylen's green ones.

He simply says, "Before you ask–because I could. What other reason can there be?" He raises up laughing, and bounds off back across the field presumably from where he came.

Coming to life, the ravens begin their usual non-melodious cawing and try to follow the canine but he is nowhere to be found, and no trace of scent remains for the red vixen to find. The creatures in attendance are befuddled.

Now however, their attention is drawn to what seems a slow spiral from above. The hawk is falling to the earth. His body hits the ground hard a short ways away, bringing up dust. Jaylen steps over to him purring and rubbing on him in comfort.

"Thank you fellow descendant. You did well. I am so sorry".

"No, for the first time in a very long life, I have helped someone. And that is a good thing to end one's life on," Amr says.

Jaylen begins her Song, hoping to make his transition as quick as possible.

To everyone's amazement instead of Amr's soul passing over, from inside the rift comes stepping out into their reality, a man. His skin is dark and smooth, his chest is bare, his loins covered in a silken draped material shimmering in the rapidly approaching evening's light. But it is his head that is the most startling even to the believer that is the Singer. For this man's head is that of a falcon. Short beaked, small black eyes set to the side of his head and great golden wings coming out of his shoulder blades in the back.

Jaylen drops to her chest in a deep bow laying her wings flat on the ground in supplication and submission to the deity before them. The Horus steps around her, gently picks up the body of the fallen Amr saying something to the little glowing ball of spirit, and together they step back into the rift. Not seconds later it pops closed and the world resumes its odd normalcy.

Story 10

A Special Singer

The tiny kitten was cold and wet. He shivered and squeaked, searching blindly for his mother's warm and comforting teat. She nuzzles the newborn into her safe belly and begins the task of cleaning and drying the tiny baby. Her rough tongue rubs him as efficiently as any towel, while she gently Sings the Song of her life and her people to him. Instilling her knowledge, values and history in the time-honored way. She knew from the moment of conception that this baby of hers would be the one of all her children to carry forth her work. The one to whom The Song would be given and shared. The Song is the passing of souls on to whatever comes next. Even she didn't know what that was; only that it was important they all go.

What makes him extra special is that he is a "he" and not a "she". Singers are traditionally female. Very few males have ever been Singers, and when they were, they are usually attributed to doing great things. One was even believed to have Sung at a unicorn's passing, but of course that is just a fanciful tale Rayla is sure. However, having seen Horus as well as the great Coyote, makes it hard to be skeptical. Nonetheless, all of her experiences, her mother's experiences, and those before them are included as she Sings her Songs to her precious baby.

Maren gambles over the stick falling, and tripping and laughing. His feet too big for his uncoordinated baby's body. Standing up, Maren shakes himself off, his still baby-blue eyes wide and full of merriment. His wings have yet to properly unfurl and feel the breeze, but at his age he only sees this as some far-off event. His mother Rayla looks on from the sunlit path in pride and approval. Her soft Song rumbling through the air as she cleans a delicate paw. She sends The Song to her last-born son without him even being conscious of it; his brain learning and memorizing it for the future, while his body runs, jumps and plays. She repeats her Song over and over. It's importance still unknown to her young kitten.

In just a few short weeks, Maren's eyes turn from baby blue to a deep green. His body grows and elongates, no longer tripping over his feet. His wings are a magnificent cascade of browns and golds, and his coat grows in full and lush. He is truly a sight to behold.

Soon Rayla will take him with her when she Sings. He has listened, now he must watch so he knows when the time is right. He needs to learn how to avoid being interrupted during his task. His choices must be decisive and quick to ensure that the soul travels safely. Not all souls go willingly. Some flit and dart around scared. Others hover over their remains unable to fathom what has happened. And some are angry and resentful at having to leave the life they knew to go somewhere they have never been.

Maren needs to learn how to Sing all of them over and with as little fuss as possible. To not get caught by humans, who have no idea of the service he will be doing for them; to not pull a soul out of a still living body too soon; to learn how to do the task he was created for. His mother needs to teach him all she knows, and all she can.

Together Maren and Rayla sit outside the home waiting for the wailing they know to signal the need for their Song. Sickness has come to this town and sadly not many are passed by. They call it the "Spanish Flu", but its name is not important. Only its grim work that needs to be tended.

This home is large, and clearly wealthy compared to many. But sickness knows not class or distance. This home will still be in need of them before the night is over. This is to be Maren's first Song. Very few males can Sing. Less than one in every century it is believed, and never has there been two male Singers at the same time, although there are dozens of female Singers around the world. No other Singer could even remember the last time a male was gifted this way.

Maren is truly special, he just didn't understand yet, *how* special. Rayla had over the years, as cats do, had many litters of kittens. Most were normal, ordinary house cats, well-loved but no trace of the gift of magic that she herself carried. She feared she would never have a Singer as she herself was getting older, and soon it would be time for her passing as well. She is well pleased with this youngster, growing up to be so handsome and big. Other Singers whom they cross paths with are amazed and fawn attention over him. They all hope to find favor with him and become his mate when he is a bit older. It's a wonderful thought to believe a whole litter could be Singers. So far Maren hasn't shown any interest in mating, his young body hasn't thickened, his head is still a bit small and his neck is still lean. But the promise is there.

Story 11

A Dragon's Tale

The cat strode down the narrow shoulder of the road as if he owned it. His paws making no sounds on the dirt. His beautiful brown and black-ticked coat gently rolling with his shoulders, hiding his equally beautiful and matching wings. All who saw him knew his self-confidence and poise were a natural thing. The quiet woods beside him gave shadow to his coat and lent a natural calmness to the air.

"Ahem," said the quiet voice from his right shoulder. "Excuse me ..."

Startled, but unwilling to show it, the cat turned

to face the voice, staring into the golden eyes of the giant creature only a scant five feet from him. Maren sat down pulling his tail around him. He settled himself for a moment, then began to wash a white paw. Not bothering to look at the odd creature he had only heard about and never before seen, he took his time to carefully clean the paw as if to dismiss the large dragon sitting mere feet in front of him. The dragon's gold and green scales help it blend into the dense trees and foliage of the surrounding woods.

Clearly the creature had been waiting for him, and manners dictated that he give the Singer time to compose himself. Maren, never one to push his luck, finally looks directly at the dragon and merely says, "Hello."

"I need to ask you for a favor," the deep rumbling voice said quietly. The cat simply blinks and waits. Even the wooded creatures seemed to settle in to listen and grow quiet, waiting to hear the conversation. The only irreverent creatures still stirring were the darn cicadas singing their song.

Although Maren felt calling it "a song" was rather demeaning compared to what he did; but to each their own. Who was he to cast aspersions when you only got topside once every 15 years or so, he thought randomly.

Interrupting his thoughts, "I am going to die soon. And I am the last of my kind here now. I need you to Sing for me, so I may cross over," says the dragon, who at this point has settled himself as well.

So as not to be towering above the little Singer as much as was reasonably possible, he was instead laying on the ground, feet widely set chest to dirt; as much eye to eye as two such disparate creatures could be.

Very un-cat like, Maren tilts his head up to the side as if deeply contemplating the request. Finally, he blinks his green eyes and replies, "I have no qualms about Singing to see you over. But there are of course a few questions. Firstly being, how do you know you are going to die soon? And how am I to necessarily find you at the time, as you are not exactly among my normal given to the task? And how do you know you are the last? I didn't believe there were any such Windriders here on this continent, yet here you are," flicking his plumed tail for emphasis. A soft breeze brings a note of cooling to the small enclave.

The dragon merely chuckles softly and replies, "We each of the great creatures have our own gifts, and sadly that is one of ours–to know the time of our own demise."

"It would be a fearsome knowledge to possess I agree," Maren's grass-green eyes blink slowly in the sun.

A pair of motorcycles fly by the unlikely pair, throwing dirt up and covering them both in a fine misted layer of road dust. The drivers never noticed the diminutive cat, and the dragon was not something they could have perceived had they looked him in the eyes. Magic had long since left almost all of the humans, and they only saw what they expected to see.

Maren stands up for a moment and shakes himself off with a quick twitch of his shoulders down to his tail.

"Then I suppose I shall see you again. What may I call you?" Maren asks. The dragon smiles, lifting the corners of its toothy mouth.

"You can call me… Elliot" And he launches himself into the air with less energy and disturbance of the ground than it would have taken the cat to jump onto a shelf. Maren watches him go and is contemplative.

Upon returning home and taking a short nap, Maren is again thinking of Elliot. Maren's mother told him the Windriders were long gone from this world and that she had never seen one. She had Sung him Songs when he was younger, of Waveriders his ancestors had met, but not Windriders. He should consider himself lucky. But he was still a cat, and so he didn't. What he did concern himself with was the thought that since this dragon was still alive, what would happen in the world and to it, once he died.

Every one of them was said to carry a part of the world's magic. He even bestirred himself to be concerned enough to wonder, would this somehow affect his Singing ability? But rapidly put that thought away as surely the world couldn't be that contrary. To lose his abilities was unthinkable.

The days came and went, turning into months but sadly the dragon was right. His final day had come. He lay on the ground, his scales no longer green nor gold but rather a single sickly shade of orange. His breathing was slow and shallow. Somehow the cat had known, and come to this place by a lovely dribble of a stream that was still unfound mostly by man.

Maren hadn't known that morning when he awakened, that this was the day of the great Windrider's passing. He had simply gotten up, checked on his human companion who was busily getting ready for another day away from home in the square steel building he called an office. He took a couple of bites in passing off the plate of food that had been lovingly set out for him. He didn't wish to be rude after all. Maren knew that if he left the plate untouched the human would worry and fret, and after a few days, pick him up and take him to that awful smelling place called a vet's. He despised that place, and distrusted those people, so it was better to take a few bites and let his companion believe all was well.

Exiting the little flap door, taking himself down the sweet-smelling cedar stairs, he begins his daily task of roaming the beautiful wooded area, meandering here and there. After a time, he felt pulled to a small glen that had this even smaller stream. It's there he sees Elliot, a shadow of his former self. The large dragon barely seems to notice the cat's approach. Maren sits himself down in front of the dragon and begins washing one of his front paws. A slit in the dragon's eye appears and he huffs a small sound of greeting.

"You came Singer. Thank you." Inclining his head, Maren puts his paw down.

"I am sorry old one. The world will be a lesser place for your passing."

Elliot, self-declared "last of the Windriders" and known by man as "dragon", closes his eye and breaths out his last long breath. The earth stills, the sky darkens a little, the stream bubbles and roils, and even the titmouse in the leaves becomes frozen as if time itself is different now.

Maren waits. Momentarily the gossamer strands that are a creature's final passings begin to float above the large physical remains. Maren stands up and spreads his soft feathered wings, opens his mouth and Sings. The air shimmers and folds in on itself to open the doorway to the next realm. But the doorway is small and this soul is large, and still seems to have a will of its own to it.

Maren strengthens his Song, pulling air into his lungs and forcing the power to the rift which opens a bit wider. For being insubstantial, this soul doesn't seem to want to go through the doorway being offered it. Maren redoubles his efforts. His wings shake and slap the air above him as if to help push the dragon's soul through. Maren almost feels as if he is flying in his attempts to move the strong-willed soul on. His front feet have left the ground in his attempt and the shadow of doubt for the first time truly enters his mind that maybe he isn't strong enough to pass this creature on.

His Song falters, allowing the rift to close slightly and the initially gossamer strands are now yellow and cream and pulsating. Closing his eyes, Maren brings his mother to mind. And his Song is her Song, and her mother's Song, and her mother's mother's Song. Combined, the power together forms a combination permitting an enlarging of the rift and helping to push the now rapidly pulsing strands into the next world. As Elliot's final transition is made, the rift snaps closed with a whiplash-like effect that drops Maren to the ground unconscious from the effort. His wings spread around him both a blanket on top and a sheet underneath.

The day wears on, but the little cat does not stir. The titmouse comes out to investigate, sniffing warily but decides that, even unresponsive, it is too much for his tiny nerves and elects to forage elsewhere. By evening Maren begins stirring. He is stiff and sore, and has a headache. He'd never had a headache before. He doesn't like the sensation. Rolling to a sphynx position, he is aware his wings are still extended and stretched, not responding to his desire to fold them. And that hurts too. He shakes himself as if wet, to bring them back into his body and they respond with only the most difficult of effort.

The dragon's body has melted into the grass and created a ring of great growth and sudden flowers. He's heard the humans call this a fairy ring, but now he knows what it really is. Shortly, Maren feels he is ready to travel and all he wants to do is go home to his warm fire and comfortable couch.

And make his way home he did, without so much as cleaning his lovely white paws or wiping the dirt off his tail. His human is very distraught when he sees the condition of his pet and makes much fuss over him that night, as it should be.

Epilogue of Sorts

Fun Cat Facts

Did you know that Sir Isaac Newton invented the cat door? It is purported that when Newton was working at the University of Cambridge, he was continually interrupted and disturbed by his cats scratching at the closed door. Calling a university carpenter, he instructed them to saw holes in the door to allow access for his pets. It is rumored that these holes can still be seen today.

🐾 🐾 🐾 🐾

Abraham Lincoln owned several cats while in the White House. And is credited with the quote, "No matter how much cats fight, there always seems to be plenty of kittens."

Ray Bradbury, the legendary science fiction writer had a deep love of cats. Cats were a constant presence while Bradbury was writing. He is credited with the saying, "I have my favorite cat, who is my paperweight, on my desk while I am writing."

Writer Ernest Hemingway was a devout cat lover who called his pets "purr factories" and "love sponges." In 1935, a ship's captain visiting Hemingway in Key West, Florida, gifted him a six-toed cat named Snowball, and soon, Snowball had populated the Hemingway estate with litters of six-toed babies carrying the polydactyl gene. Hemingway named them after popular celebrities of his time and decades later, over 50 of Snowball's mutant descendants still reside at the Hemingway home-turned-museum, in Key West, Florida.

While it is commonly thought that the ancient Egyptians were the first to domesticate cats, the oldest known pet cat was recently found in a 9,500-year-old grave on the Mediterranean island of

Cyprus. This grave predates early Egyptian art, depicting cats by 4,000 years or more.

During the time of the Spanish Inquisition, Pope Innocent VIII condemned cats as evil and thousands of cats were burned. Unfortunately, the widespread killing of cats led to an explosion of the rat population, which exacerbated the effects of the Black Death.

Cats are North America's most popular pet.

A cat's brain is biologically more similar to our human brain than it is to a dog's. Both humans and cats have identical regions in their brains that are responsible for emotions.

A cat typically has about 12 whiskers on each side of its face.

In the original Italian version of Cinderella, the benevolent fairy godmother was a cat.

For your love of cats, check out our other non-fiction works anywhere books are sold online. Titles include:

The Siberian Cat

and

The Raw Facts of Feline Feeding.

Turn the page for an exciting preview of the all-new, original story of werewolves and zombies in today's world.

Time of the Wolf

by Alice E Wright

Catch it in 2023 at all online retailers!

Time of the Wolf

Chapter 1

Damn, damn, damn there's one here. I can smell it. Heaving a heavy sigh, I look around and assess my surroundings. The coffee shop is jammed full of customers this morning. At least a dozen. Plus, the four working behind the counter. This could get ugly if this thing goes full zombie in here. My mate and partner is out in the car. Picking up my phone I text Ellan, telling her the situation. She responds right away, "So what's our play?"

"Your call," I respond. "Let's just get our coffee, pull back and watch. Too many in here to sort."

"Fine with me but I really wanted to go to Costco today damn it."

"We may still have time." Even as I reply to the text, I can feel her rolling her eyes at my response.

When it's my turn to order, I have located and identified which patron is the Myrna. He's waiting for his order, scrolling through his cell phone's feed; as calm and placid as any other customer.

Texting my wife again with the fellow's description, we fall into a comfortable pattern of following the soon-to-turn zombie Myrna. Ellan drives, with me hurriedly undressing in the back of the van, being sure to remove all of my clothing. Especially my leather belt. Those really suck when you are shifting forms if you don't get them off in time!

It takes me around 15 minutes these days to fully shift to my wolf form, and sadly it will be a couple of hours before I am able to shift back once we complete the kill. Sucks getting old.

My wolf form is grizzled and gray but the two-hundred and fifty pounds of me is on the larger end of the spectrum. My browns and grays are well suited to the Arizona desert. Even the slash of white across my face tends to blend in well with light and shadow.

"Are you ready honey?" She asks over her shoulder from the driver's seat. I give her ear a quick whiffling nuzzle in response. We have followed the Myrna for what seems like a really long time down a freeway and through city streets. Most of these things can't hold a pattern that long. Not sure what that says about this one.

Finally, he pulls into a mostly empty parking lot. The building looks closed for the weekend. Deliberately getting out of the car, our target walks slowly to the double glass doors, phone in one hand, coffee in the other. He stands there for at least a full two minutes, scrolling through his phone while sipping his coffee, now and again pulling on an obviously locked set of doors.

Suddenly, he drops both his coffee and his phone. There seems to be an audible pause as we watch the scene unfold. Placidly staring at the doors' ends when he grabs both handles and begins shaking them violently, pulling and screaming like the proverbial banshee.

"That's our cue" Ellan says exiting our vehicle.

I follow behind her coming through the break between the front seats and out the door she has left open for me.

We split up, Ellan walking slowly towards the now-maddened Myrna, me staying off to the side.

Ellan starts whistling and clapping to attract its attention. He turns to look at what the noise and distraction is. His pupils no longer react to light, his clothes look slept in now that I can see him more clearly. Taking the bait, he charges across the parking lot at her. His single-minded focus is on my wife, while completely ignoring my slow silent steps. Around the halfway point, Ellan is still making noise and waving her arms to draw his attention but she starts backing up and I begin my short dash. Getting in close, from the side I launch myself at the moving target clamping my jaws tightly in a full-mouth bite on this newly-turned Myrna zombie's neck. I crush flesh and bone with my bite into a mangled mess. It never saw me and together we collapse into a heap on the rapidly-warming Arizona asphalt.

Sometimes it can take a few minutes for the brain

to cease functioning and during that time it is very dangerous for us. We are crushing the entire neck and spinal column to prevent this thing from getting up and killing everyone in its path, while these things are trying to return the favor and rip the werewolf into many ribboned pieces. Feeling my teeth close together, I give a hard shake to be sure the spinal column is well and truly severed.

Ellan walks up to us looking us over. She's looking for bites on me and to make sure this thing is no longer moving.

Smirking she says, "I think you got him." Releasing my hold, I step back; my muzzle and most of my neck now lightly covered in the stinking black gore that a Myrna's blood congeals into.

"You know, it's at times like this that I wish we could high five." I raise my paw and she laughs.

"Hey let's call this in and get you cleaned up."

I agree. I haven't closed my jaws or licked my lips, and I keep my head down so none of the foul gore rolls down my throat.

We walk back to the van and Ellan lifts the back

hatch, taking a cooler of clean water out placing it on the ground for me to wash my head and neck in.

A security vehicle drives up for the company or building, I'm not sure which at this point, and looks at the body then glances at me cleaning off the mess in the cooler. He makes a few notations on an electronic memo stick and drives off. Definitely a rent-a-cop, as most off-duty police officers stop and chat for a while.

Soon the lime-green emergency services vehicle pulls into the parking lot. Randy, one of the state's more well-known and liked technicians, steps out of the agency's repurposed ambulance used by most local governmental agencies these days. His friendly, easy demeanor makes him appreciated and well-liked among both the werewolf teams as well as the survivors whom he is partially responsible for notifying of their former loved one's demise.

"Hey Ellan, you didn't call for a cleanup crew so they just sent me".

"We're good Randy, thanks. It went down clean

today," handing over her government issued identicard for him to scan and tag to this specific kill and subsequent payment to their account. He scans the card and returns it to her while I come around from the back of the van still dripping wet, but now only from water and not black goo.

"Hey old man," Randy greets me. I lift my lip exposing a single eye tooth, in a mock snarl falling into our comfortable routine. Smiling, Randy pulls on his nitrile gloves from the depths of a pocket and turns to begin the normally grim task of positive identification of the remains, including confirmation of Myrna status.

Picking up the dead man's hand, he runs the specialized memo stick over the back of the hand and down fingers confirming both fingerprints as well as vascular mapping for a positive ID. We only get paid when those get confirmed and then synced up with our scanned ID. This was a clean and textbook kill. Easy money. But even with that, it is never without some inherent risk to both partners;

hence, why it is mandated that wolves only work in teams of two but no more than three. Not that we generally allow mandates to be dictated to us. But it's a smart idea, and as such has merit we adhere to.

"We all good? Can we go now?"

Looking over at us, "Sure, he's all set and tagged. But do me a solid. I am obviously by myself; can you help me load this up?" Ellan turns and opens the side door of the van, allowing me to hop in to escape the rising temperature; turning around I lay down to watch my wife and Randy work.

It's good to get out of the rapidly warming Arizona day, the heat is hard on me, and on werewolves in general.

"Of course," she responds. Being on the other side of fifty has never stopped her from the heavy work and as she walks over, tells him, "Happy to help, but you get the gooey end!" They smirk and together get the two-hundred-pound corpse picked up and moved into the containment box still in the back of the vehicle.

"You know, that damn thing has wheels. We

could have just brought it to the body," Ellan says, not really upset, just a bit out of breath from moving a dead (pun intended) weight almost seventy feet.

"Yeah well, where's the fun in that?"

"Uh-huh" she huffs in mock displeasure. Randy busies himself with the requirements of his job while Ellan returns to the van closing the back hatch after dumping the cooler and returning it to its place to be cleaned and refilled at home. She returns to the driver's seat, making sure the back air conditioner is blowing well. She always looks after me.

Looking at me in the rear-view mirror she grins, "At least I get to finish my coffee, this stuff is expensive! Ha-ha!" Putting the vehicle in gear and settling her sunglasses on, she drives us home, knowing I will need about another hour or so before I can successfully shift back to human.

Once home, I lay on the comforter thrown carelessly across the bed. I am an old wolf, fairly newly-turned, in the scheme of things. My grizzled muzzle, now clean of the morning's gore, rests on my paws while I follow my mate with all my senses.

I worry for her. Meaning, when I should pass on.

Though not an Alpha or even a second, I am still far-enough in the middle of the pack's status to ensure some young pup will be quick to try taking advantage of my encroaching infirmities. But then, my mate will be sure to dissuade any advantage-seekers, at least for a while. This brings a smile to my eyes. She is as dominant as they come. More so than even the local Alpha, and this made our lives together never without conflict or easy, but I love her just the same.

I enjoy watching her in the shower. The water cascading down her while she carelessly washes the job's dirt, grime and gore away. In her human guise she is tall with long brown hair and green eyes. A few more wrinkles these days, not as taught and firm, and maybe if I am honest, her hair is more gray than brown really … but she's mine as I am hers.

Wolves don't live forever, far from it. The same diseases that afflict humans afflict the wolves. Heart disease, arthritis, cancers ... all of it. More slowly it was true, and sometimes didn't that suck more? But nonetheless, we are ravaged by time as every other creature on this earth eventually is.

My wife is younger than me by a decade or so but has had some hard fights in her time, given her scars and not quite healed wounds that I know still pain her.

She finishes her shower in due time and begins towel-drying herself. I close my eyes to just enjoy listening to the normal sounds from within the house. The soft cotton of the towel rubbing against her body. The bathroom fan running softly in a vain attempt to keep the moisture at bay. Birds outside the oversized French doors flittering and chirping eagerly at the full feeders and of course the various hum of electronics from within the house itself.

I keep a close eye on my mate and husband. I worry for him. Liam is getting older, slower and less responsive to threats. Even when I changed him, I knew it wasn't a cure-all, that time was not on his side. His heart was bad and he was out of other options. And it was not technically a sanctioned turning by the local pack Alpha. But I love him and wasn't ready for him to leave me yet. I feel I need to protect him during the hunts now, but of course he wouldn't see it that way.

I have witnessed a couple of wolves who had been bitten during the early Myrna zombie hunts, and it was not good. It took almost an entire pack and a sharp shooter to ultimately bring the bitten werewolves down. But not before a lot of damage had been done. Innocents had been killed, pack members had been maimed, and of course in today's world it had all been filmed for the newest social media craze to bandy their ever-shrill cry to call all wolves a danger to society.

Demand for a national identification system along with public websites, like those for sex offenders, was always a favorite topic in the news. It hadn't been easy to calm the craze from the last one. I love my mate too much to permit such a thing to happen to him, or our family. Fully dressed now, I pick up my keys and say, "I'm still going to Costco".